THE
L

Marele Day grew up in Sydney and graduated from Sydney University with BA (Hons). Her work experience ranges from fruit picking to academic teaching, and she is currently a freelance editor. She has travelled extensively and lived in Italy, France and Ireland. Travels include a voyage by yacht from Cairns to Singapore which resulted in near shipwreck in the Java Sea. THE LIFE AND CRIMES OF HARRY LAVENDER is her first novel.

The Life and Crimes of Harry Lavender

Marele Day

CORONET BOOKS
Hodder and Stoughton

First published in Great Britain in 1994
First published in paperback in 1994
by Hodder and Stoughton
A division of Hodder Headline PLC

A Coronet paperback

British Library Cataloguing in Publication Data

Day, Marele
  Life and Crimes of Harry Lavender. – New ed
  I. Title
823.914 [F]

ISBN 0 340 61346 7

Printed and bound in Great Britain by
Cox & Wyman Ltd, Reading, Berkshire

Hodder and Stoughton
A division of Hodder Headline PLC
338 Euston Road
London NW1 3BH

I woke up feeling like death. Ironically appropriate, given what the day held in store. White light poured in, even before I opened my eyes and a variety of sounds, all too loud. Someone was pounding my brain like a two year old who's just discovered a hammer. In between blows I managed to prise open the eyes. Close by the bed was a bottle of Jack Daniels: empty. And an ash tray: full. Clothes were strewn all over the place and through the french doors roared the sights and sounds of Sydney. As I got out of bed I realised I wasn't the only one in it. There was a good looking blond in there as well. I didn't recall issuing the invitation but I must have. No one gets into my room, let alone my bed, without one.

Out in the kitchen the naked light bulb bravely competed with the glare of the day. There was another ash tray full of butts, two glasses and a bowl of olives and cockroaches, sardonic little reminders of the night before. After a couple of unsuccessful attempts I managed to light the gas under the coffee and, closing the stable door after the horse had bolted, crammed a handful of vitamins down my throat.

The coffee revived me a little, a hot then cold shower even more. The blond slept on, unperturbed by my rummaging through the clothes on the floor looking for something suitable to wear. Thank God the black suit was hanging in the wardrobe neatly pressed. The black shoes were where I'd apparently left them the night before – one in the waste paper bin and the other on the mantelpiece. I dressed and took a long hard look at myself in the mirror. As long as I didn't start haemorrhaging from the eyes things would be all right. I grabbed the dark glasses. Just in case.

'Time to go sweetheart,' I whispered into the blond's aural orifice. Not a flicker of an eyelid or a murmur. Next time I shook him. 'C'mon mate, wake up. I've got to go to a funeral.'

We were at Taylor Square before I remembered the flowers. 'Just stop here a minute,' I instructed the driver as the cab swung round into Flinders Street. My heels clattered across the street and stopped on the safe ground of the median strip while my finger jabbed uselessly at the pedestrian button. The deroes who frequented that small triangle of threadbare green had neatly folded up their newspapers and had started in on their liquid breakfasts. I scanned their faces as I always did, looking for a face I would no longer recognise, one that would no longer recognise mine. They didn't look twice. I was part of the other world, though this morning I felt decidedly part of theirs. Perhaps they had the answer: never get sober.

The flower shop was near Kinselas, an elegant night spot that used to be a funeral parlour but where people now ate devilled kidneys and crumbed brains in the former chapel and afterwards went upstairs for the show. My own brain being in the state it was that morning I didn't even think about Kinselas' former status till I noticed the flower shop so conveniently close by. Memories are short in this city and facades change all the time. It was not the first time I'd visited that particular florist: once, seven years ago, I bought flowers there. For my own wedding, if you can call a five minute session at the Registry Office a wedding.

I pointed to a bunch of violets and held out a ten dollar note. Somehow the colour of violets seemed appropriate.

'Card?' the same woman asked, her social patter down to a bare minimum.

'No,' I replied, matching her word for word. And walked back to the cab where the meter was clocking up the day's expenses.

I'd met the departed a couple of times. He was Marilyn Bannister's young brother. I had not seen Marilyn since school and indeed it was another school friend who'd given her my number. I was glad to know the old girls' network was still is force though Sydney is pretty much like that anyway. Not what you know but who you know. Without contacts in this city you'd be dead. And sometimes dead even with them.

6

So Marilyn contacted me. I was in a slack period, doing insurance surveillance and boring the pants off myself. I had enough self control to let the phone ring six times before answering.

'Claudia Valentine speaking.'

The caller identified herself as Marilyn Edwards. The name meant nothing. Then she told me we'd been at school together and gave another surname: Bannister.

My mind flicked through the past and dragged Marilyn Bannister out. The girl no one had wanted to sit next to, the girl without the Colgate ring of confidence.

'Marilyn! How are you?'

She didn't want to talk about her health, she wanted to meet me.

'Just a minute, I'll check with my secretary.' Silently I counted to ten then spoke into the phone again. 'It seems to be all right for later on this afternoon, Marilyn.' . . . 'The Regent? Five-thirty? Fine. I'll meet you in the foyer.'

Men in uniform with gold braid directed cabs and stretched limos in and out of the curved driveway. The automatic doors opened and I was suitably impressed with the thirteenth best hotel in the world. No other Australian hotel even made it to the top fifty. I wondered whether it wasn't some international joke ranking the only Australian hotel in the top fifty thirteenth. Because of the superstition in the industry most hotels don't even have a thirteenth floor.

The clientele was well heeled and well coiffed, the Americans well heeled and the Japanese well coiffed. The foyer was a large open plan affair with lounge chairs specifically designed for fat cats. I curled myself up in one of them, more cat-like than fat, and waited. But not for long. At 5.30 precisely a woman in an expensive linen suit entered and made a beeline towards me.

'You haven't changed a bit,' she said.

She had. Considerably. She'd lost about 10 kilos, the braces were gone, and a lot of money had been spent on grooming. But beneath the make-up the face was taut and drawn. People

7

rarely came to private investigators with good news.

'Shall we go upstairs?' she said crisply indicating the mezzanine.

Above the greenery dripping copiously from the mezzanine was a row of tables with black glass tops and chairs even more spacious than the ones in the foyer. A waiter silently appeared and presented us with a cocktail menu. In the centre of the table was a large goblet of mixed unsalted nuts. Marilyn's exterior was as cool as her white dress but in the lap of that dress she was shredding up Kleenex.

'Do you remember my brother Mark?'

'Sure I do. Is he in trouble?'

She swallowed quite a large quantity of air and extended her palms in a gesture of helplessness.

'He's . . . he's . . .'

I knew the word she couldn't speak and leant across and touched her arm.

'The police say it was natural causes.'

'But you don't think so.'

'No,' she said firmly.

Of all the roads that converged on Taylor Square, Flinders Street was the quickest way out of the city to the slow sprawl of suburbs. It was also the road to the cemetery. The old terrace houses built for workers when this was the outskirts of Sydney Town gave way to playing fields, beyond that the Showground and Cricket Ground, and closer, right on the road, the twin schools: Sydney Girls' High and Sydney Boys' High. It was ten minutes to lunchtime and the schools were quiet at this time of day, the girls in brown and yellow furiously studying science in the new wing and Latin in the old, the boys in brown and blue doing the same.

I remembered that little blond kid in brown and blue standing at the bus stop mucking around with his mates, remembered Marilyn whispering that he had come top of English in his first exam, whispering because being good at English meant being a wimp, though the word then was sissy.

Now he was dead.

The lights changed and the taxi driver honked his horn.

'C'mon mate,' he shouted at the car in front, 'they're not going to get any greener!'

Along this road to the cemetery my life unravelled. After the high school the next landmark was the university where I spent four years getting an Arts degree. With honours. It didn't mean much in the real world but it had at least taught me how to do research. It was not unlike what I was doing now except it had been behind a desk instead of a steering wheel and the library had expanded to take in the whole city. The campus had still not acquired 'character', and remained a hodgepodge of buildings, 'landscaped' with the mean type of vegetation that thrives on sandy soil.

Further down the road, past impersonal shopping centres and red roofed houses, was my primary school. It was lunchtime now and the playground was alive with squeals and banana sandwiches. I saw the child I used to be, the girl too tall for her age, the girl with no father, beg me with the sad eyes of childhood. I turned away from the memory and instead watched for Mark's funeral procession. There was none. Like choko and passionfruit vines, funeral processions have disappeared from the streets of Sydney.

Mark had been found dead on the floor beside his computer table. The autopsy report had given the cause of death as cardiac arrest. The pacemaker had missed a few beats.

A pacemaker? In a young guy like that?

'It's not unheard of,' said Marilyn. 'We knew of someone else Mark's age, an Iron Man. He . . . he also died.'

A spanner in the works. The hi-tech heart spasming out of control.

'I don't know if I can help, Marilyn, I'm an investigator, not a doctor.'

'I've been to the doctor. What I came to see you about, Claudia, is this.'

She handed me an envelope, lightweight and neatly sliced open. It was addressed to Marilyn and inside was a card, which simply said in thick black letters:

TERMINAL ILLNESS

We drove through the double gates and the cab crunched to a halt. There were a couple of chapels and one step closer to heaven was the red brick chimney of the crematorium. A crowd had gathered already: one group consisted of sunburnt boys in dark suits and sneakers, the other of artistically garbed young men and women trying to convince each other, with bursts of conversation that dropped to the ground like pebbles, that they were all still immortal.

At the centre of this group was a face that could launch ships. A luxuriant mane of black hair overshadowed the face as white as porcelain, the only spot of colour a blood red cupid's bow mouth. Sporadically she burst into tears and waved away arms that went round her shoulders in sympathy.

Tough and histrionic.

Another group consisted of Marilyn, a grey haired couple and two small boys making train tracks in the pebbles with sticks. In the parking lot two guys sat dumbly in an unmarked BMW. They looked like cops. Or hired muscle. I took note of the registration number and walked over to Marilyn.

'Claudia, this is my mother and father.' The grey haired man shook my hand vigorously. 'Claudia is . . . an old school friend.'

'Glad you could come, dear,' said her mother.

I bent down to the two boys playing in the gravel. They were about the same age as my own two kids.

'Oh, these are my boys, Mark and Jeremy.'

'Hi!' I said.

'Whatta you got them flowers for?' asked the smaller one.

'They're for your Uncle Mark.'

'He's dead. He got dead in an accident.'

The innocent mouths of babes.

'Yes,' I said, 'It's sad isn't it?'

'Yeah. Do you wanna play trains with us?'

I placed my wilting bunch of violets up the front with the other flowers arranged in wreaths or bunches. There were roses and carnations. And there was lavender.

The surfer boys carried the coffin past the rows of family and friends. The BMW guys had not entered the chapel.

The ceremony was brief. Someone said a few complimentary things about the deceased, a promising talent whose death would leave a blank page in the book of Australian Literature. There were a few soft moans about the metaphor but nothing compared to Mrs Bannister's uncontrollable sobbing when the organist played Mark's favourite song.

It was Lou Reed's 'Walk on the Wild Side'.

When we came out into the sunlight the BMW was gone. Marilyn bundled her kids into the car then headed towards me.

'Thanks, Claudia, Mum and Dad appreciated your coming. I don't think they were overly impressed with the rest of the gathering.'

There might never be another occasion to have all Mark's friends together in one place.

'I don't suppose by any chance your parents have invited them back for a wake, have they?'

'No,' she said shortly. 'Apparently they're all going to the Imperial for a drink.'

'You going?'

'I've got to get the boys back. I'm passing by that way if you want a lift.'

'Thanks,' I said, getting into the car. 'Did you happen to notice those two men in the BMW?'

'Yes,' she said, swinging the car out onto Bunnerong Road.

'Do you know them?'

'No. Never seen them before. They don't look like the sort

of people Mark would know but then . . .'

'Could have been cops. They usually come for a look if it's homicide.'

Her hands tightened on the steering wheel. Then I remembered: as far as the cops were concerned Mark died of natural causes.

The Imperial was by no means imperial even with the renovations that had taken place since I'd last seen it aeons ago. It had a carpet now and the lights were dim. The pool tables were gone and in their place were games machines and a video juke-box. Above the bar an inaudible TV provided some diverting flickers of light. A few gentlemen in shorts and navy blue singlets stood at the bar, hangovers from the days when most pubs looked and smelled like public lavatories in all their tiled glory. The sunburnt boys all sat at one table and Mark's trendier set of friends at another.

I walked up to the bar and ordered a Scotch.

'Make that two.' I turned to see one of the surfer boys grinning at me. I grinned back.

'I'm Robbie.'

'Claudia.'

He only came up to my shoulder but so do most people. 'You a relative?'

'No. A friend of the family. I knew Mark when he was a kid.'

'He was a good bloke.'

Robbie steered me over to his table and introduced me around. Johnno, Thommo, they all seemed to have names ending in o. Most of the ties were off now and stuffed into top pockets.

'Well old Mark finally went down the pipeline.'

'Yeah, he was a good bloke.'

'What was he like?' I ventured.

'He was a good bloke.'

I rephrased the question so as to get an answer that consisted of more than just 'good' and 'bloke'.

'What sort of things was he into?'

One of them sniggered and tossed his head in the direction of the ship launcher. But his voice said something different.

'Surfing. Like us.'

'That all?'

'Video games. He played them at home.'

Now it was my turn to toss my head.

'He had machines like that at home?'

The tough nut doing all the talking looked at me as if I was a moron.

'Naa, he played games on his computer.'

'He was onto a goldmine there,' said another member of the party. 'Did yez check out the sound system? Pretty neat stuff, eh? Wish I had a sugar-daddy giving me presents like that.'

'Wonder what the payoff was. Wonder if he had to . . .'

Robbie had had enough. 'Will you guys shut up! You know it wasn't like that, it was just payment for writing a book.'

'Mark never told us he was writing a book,' someone mumbled.

'I'm not surprised, the way you guys carry on. Just because you're writing a book doesn't mean you're a poofter!'

That shut them up. The silence was full of youthful nonchalance. Dedicated hedonists, all so cool, unaware that sooner or later the debt collector would be around, knocking hard on their bodies.

But I wanted them to keep talking.

'You guys play video games?'

'Yeah, we play sometimes, when there's no surf.'

There was a communal snigger. I'd stumbled across an injoke.

'Anyone like a game now?'

'I'm game,' said Robbie quick as a flash.

The rest of them sat there grinning at me. I guessed they didn't know too many women who weren't blond and who were over twenty five and still alive.

We put our money in the slot and the bright little shapes of spaceships appeared on the screen. Robbie went first. It seemed the little red thing had to explode as many of the

13

multicoloured shapes as it could before the little white flecks of light exploded the red thing.

'OK, your turn,' said Robbie confidently.

The targets came up on the screen and I took the red knobbed handle in one hand and started jabbing at the button with the other.

'Who was Mark writing this book for?' I asked.

'Wouldn't have a clue. He didn't talk about that kind of stuff with the guys. All he told me was that someone was paying him to write a book and that he'd given him a computer.'

'When was the last time you saw Mark?'

'About a month ago. We went round to his place, hadn't seen him at the beach so we thought we'd drop in on him. He seemed a bit paranoid. You know, kinda looking over his shoulder all the time. See, there was this knock on the door and he jumped. I mean his arse physically left the chair. Then he goes, "Who is it?" Like he's expecting the Mafia or something. But it was only Sally, forgotten her keys.'

'Sally?'

'Over there. His girlfriend, Sally Villos. You must have noticed her, she has a way of drawing attention to herself. By the way,' he said, looking at the screen, 'you've bombed out.'

'You can't win them all,' I said, emulating the youthful nonchalance. 'How well do you know her?'

'As well as I want to. She didn't hang out with us. She's at NIDA or art college or something. A bit up herself.'

'I'd like to meet her.'

'**C**ome and join the party!' said Sally once the informal formalities were over. 'Here's to Mark,' and she downed yet another Tequila Sunrise.

Her friends looked a little uncomfortable but she kept on drinking. So did I. I was working on the hair of the dog theory and my little dog was the long-haired type. Besides, there was something about Sally that made you want to drink. She had the nerve-buckling quality of the neurotic. Flashing out beta waves that sucked at your force field. She was bereaved. Of course. And she was making sure everyone knew it. Centre stage now, her head turned to the light, eyes open wide so the tears wouldn't spill out onto the make-up. She had an audience around her who all 'understood'.

'Why? . . . Why?' Her eyes clutched at my face but there was no answer there. Not yet anyway.

'It wasn't the stuff, it was safe, he said it was, he didn't want to die, he wanted to live, to . . . to . . . *do everything* . . .' I think I knew what 'stuff' she was talking about and apparently I wasn't the only one.

One of the beautiful young men stood up and took her drink away: 'C'mon Sally, it's time to go.'

'Just where do you get off, Justin?' she said, fixing him with those beautiful castrating eyes.

Her arm, young as a child's, reached across the table towards the Tequila Sunrise and made contact with the glass. But the contact was too brusque and the Sunrise spread blood red along the horizon of the table.

She watched the dripping colours die, her eyes widening with horror. Slowly, slowly it began, the dawning realisation. Up, up it came, till it reached its peak.

'Nooooooo!' she howled.

The 'wake' was over.

Do you remember my brother Mark? Sure I do. Is he in trouble? He's . . . he's . . . The police say it was natural causes. But you don't think so. No. What was the official cause of death? Cardiac arrest. Did he have problems with his heart? Yes. He had a pacemaker. It's not unheard of. We knew of someone else Mark's age, an Iron Man. He . . . he also died. What was actually wrong with his heart? It was congenital: a hole in the heart. I don't know if I can help, Marilyn, I'm an investigator, not a doctor. I've been to the doctor. What I came to see you about, Claudia, is this. I already felt . . . you see as well as the heart the autopsy . . . there was heroin. They found heroin in the bloodstream.

Not enough to kill him but . . . We had no idea, no idea, that's why I felt . . . if there was that what else was there, what else was there about my brother . . . When was the last time you saw him? A few months ago. He didn't keep in touch much. Specially lately. Dad was always on at him about getting a job and suddenly he announces he has one. Commissioned to write 'the best seller of the century' as he put it. Who commissioned him? Yes, well we asked him that and he became quite cryptic. 'You'll see when it comes out.' And that was all? That was all. What about the heroin, what did the police have to say about that? They asked us about it but of course we couldn't tell them anything. I don't know if they made further enquiries but the eventual finding was no suspicious circumstances surrounding the death.

I pressed the stop button. I didn't know when I bought it that this little pocket cassette recorder would be so handy. You could even switch it on by remote control as long as the control wasn't too remote. A little something I'd picked up in the States where I'd spent some time licking my wounds after The Divorce and sleepwalking my way through a number of self defence programs ranging from tai chi to karate. It was through karate I'd met Wali and Kemal, otherwise known as Sol and Ken. They were born again Sufis at night and 'efficiency experts' during the day. What this meant was that they were spies for the hotel industry. With the go-ahead of the management they would book into a large hotel as guests. They'd watch what was going on, get into casual conversation with other guests and hotel staff, nodding, smiling, agreeing, and all the time their little pocket cassettes would be recording and recording. Like a native with beads, I was impressed as hell with this little gadget. In those days when the future fanned out in front of me, I was going to use it to write a book. But here I was, just like Ken and Sol, recording conversations in hotels. They saw nothing incongruous about their daytime lives as Sol and Ken and their Sufi lives as Wali and Kemal. This was San Francisco in the early eighties still trying to live the dreams of the sixties and seventies. Back in

Sydney I saw nothing incongruous about nights of boozing and days of workouts. Sydney was like San Francisco in many ways except that in Sydney the weirdos didn't carry guns.

There was a knock on the door. Jack.

'This came for you today, one of those Interflora deliveries.'

It was a potplant.

'Coming down for a drink?'

'No thanks, Jack, I've got a bottle under the bed in a brown paper bag.'

'OK, see you in the morning.'

It was a potplant of lavender. Wrapped in purple tissue paper with thin shiny ribbon. With a card: 'To my Valentine.'

I glowed inside. Then the glow turned to smoulder. It was not February 14, it was not even February.

Then the glow came back again, gently lifting the corners of my mouth. Last night's blond. He'd remembered my name even if I couldn't remember his.

I sat out on the balcony and listened to the night. Downstairs in the public bar was the faint clunk of Jack putting the chairs up. There was wind in the trees and the occasional swish of a car. Once I heard the putt putt of a boat crossing the harbour. In between times I made a mental list of things to do tomorrow. It was a beautiful night, the kind of night when lovers walk in the park by the water and grow limpid as the shimmering lights. It was a dangerous night to be on your own.

I closed the french doors and got into bed. The last thing I remember before drifting to sleep was the drowsy smell of lavender.

I dream of funerals. My own. It is a state occasion and I am laid out in the open box moving slowly through the streets of Sydney. The buildings are tall reflective glass. It is my image that is reflected in that glass.

I am famous, a legend in my time. All of Sydney has turned out to pay homage, I have done so much for so many. I smile. Idle curiosity passes for homage in the press. The people hold sprigs of lavender, like rosemary on Anzac Day. Rosemary for remembrance, lavender for . . . me. They will remember me. At the going down of the city's son and in the mourning they will remember.

Police hold the crowds back, allowing the entourage smooth passage. I smile. In death as in life the police allow me smooth passage. I can see everything. The Premier is there and all my friends. Even my enemies are friends now. The media too, filming faces in the crowd, members of the entourage respectfully lowering their heads or adjusting their hats with face-obscuring gestures. Strange bedfellows will be framed in those photographs, to be later indulged in by the press. A blackmailer would have a field day.

Collier takes notes, for the obituary. The End of an Era. It is already on the newsstands, my name in thick purple letters. Not black. Purple. There is no mistake. In the dream I can smell it.

I wake from this dream with the same coffin smile.

Then there is the other dream I wake from suffocating, drowning in rubble. But it is my body crumbling, not the city. It can never be destroyed, it will grow and spread exactly as I have planned it. They will remember me. Oh yes, they will remember.

'**B**ernie? It's Claudia.'

I waited while Bernie went through his routine.

'Shut up, Bernie. I've got one for you: a BMW.' I gave him the registration number.

'Busy! How can you be busy? You're a public servant, aren't you?' ... 'OK. This afternoon. Leave it on the answering machine if I'm not there, all right?' ... 'Thought you'd be used to talking to machines by now. See ya later, Bernie, and have a nice day,' I added in my best American accent.

I heard the inevitable cop-you-later and sighed. One of these days he was going to use that disgusting excuse for a pun on someone who'd punch his head in. Probably wouldn't stop him though. Bernie was irrepressible.

I could easily have got to the Motor Registry Office through the front door. Anyone can get access to the names cars are registered in as long as they have a good reason and three weeks to wait. I didn't have either. But I did have Bernie.

I took the bus into the city. The Daimler was being tuned and I welcomed the opportunity to take a ten minute ride with no worries about parking. Besides, I spent so much time watching and waiting in the car it sometimes felt like I lived in it.

The bus was nearly empty apart from a few odd people who, like me, live outside the nine to five routine – a couple of old girls with shopping bags and tightly permed blue hair, a young mum with toddlers and a group of old blokes who got on fumbling with their concession passes. 'Eh, Charlie, down the back,' called one of them. And they all went down the back, grinning like truant schoolboys.

We passed the Glebe Island Container Terminal.

21

Terminal illness. Terminal. Term in an illness. The combinations and permutations. I was on my way to investigate one of them right now. And here was another one.

Rows of containers, a giant's building blocks, innocuous in their uniformity. Terminal illness. Terminal containers. I'd seen one yesterday: Mark's coffin. Transported from this world into the next. I wondered about the contents of these huge containers, wondered how many kilos of heroin were down there right this minute. Life-terminating containers. Police estimate the amount of drugs apprehended is only 10 per cent of the whole. Not counting the amount that sticks to their greasy palms. Too wide yet but not to be dismissed. Start with what's close. First the terminal. Then the illness. The closest thing to Mark's dead body was the computer. And closer still, in the dead heart of the body, was the pacemaker.

We wound through Pyrmont, then suddenly: the city. The tall blocks of buildings, the centre pole of Sydney Tower that dazzled the city with fool's gold at sunset but was somewhat sallow at this time of day. Not quite the metropolis of New York but still it took your breath away, so much of it, so suddenly. Now we were on the Expressway over Darling Harbour where buildings with the eyes gouged out had been demolished to make way for 'development', for the men of power to build monoliths to themselves. Some days the city looked like a huge building site. The present annihilating the past and sweet-talking the future. We ducked under the Monorail, that stealthy snake-like creature that had lately insinuated itself into the city, passed docks and piers and luxury launches with names like *The Great Gatsby, Sea Princess, Sea Empress,* and the old warehouses that reminded you that Sydney was, after all, a port. Then the row of brick buildings, the back of them at least, that my eye always followed, with outside metal stairs zigzagging across them like the ones you saw in old movies where cops chased robbers. Instead of the cops and robbers here a banana palm grew.

The bus turned off the Expressway and up into the city's pulsing heart.

I walked along York Street towards the computer shop. At night along here there were cockroaches big as rats but now they were lulled to sleep in their subterranean beds by the metal-and-flesh traffic.

'Is Otto in today?' I asked the three eager young men in schoolboy ties and brilliant white shirts.

'Sure. Otto!'

Otto came out from the back with a cup of coffee in one hand and a ham and cheese croissant in the other. He was chewing and there were little bits of flaky pastry caught in his beard.

'Claudia!' he said, pronouncing my name like a cloud.

'Can we talk?' There were no customers and besides, Otto rarely dealt with customers, or clients as he was continually correcting me. He was the technical expert and talked to machines.

'Of course. Come to my office.'

I took a bite of his croissant and accepted the offer of coffee.

'You know the joke about the computer operator who died of a terminal illness? Well it's not a joke any more.'

I showed him the card, and filled him in on the circumstances of the death, including the pacemaker. I didn't mention the heroin, it wasn't Otto's department. But computers were.

'Hmm, the pacemaker,' he said narrowing his eyes. 'I don't know, it's not my department. As far as I know they are absolutely reliable. Perhaps in the connection to the heart . . .'

Ah yes, the slender thread between the fallible and the infallible.

I'm going to pay a visit to his flat tonight. Check out the scene of the crime, you might say, particularly the computer. Interested?'

M y appointment with Dr Mackintosh was at 2 pm. The surgery was up the driveway of a neat little cottage built sometime in the thirties, as was most of Maroubra. There were racks of *National Geographic* and *New Idea*, and a box of toys that a sniffly kid was rummaging in. I looked at the people waiting and wondered what was wrong with them, as they were no doubt wondering about me. None of them looked like abortion candidates, or drug addicts either, though I knew at least one of Dr Mackintosh's patients had done heroin. I wondered if Dr Mackintosh knew.

The door opened and a tall gentleman wearing glasses appeared. 'Mrs Loukakis?' 'Costas, come,' said the mother of the sniffly kid. 'Put it back in the box.' The child's mouth turned down at the corners and his bottom lip bulged. 'It's all right, Mrs Loukakis, he can bring it in with him.' Costas rearranged his mouth and beamed at the nice doctor who ushered them in and closed the door.

I picked the one *New Idea* that didn't have royalty on the cover and flicked idly through the well worn pages. There was a half done crossword that I proceeded to finish. I preferred cryptic crosswords but there was nothing cryptic about *New Idea*. I liked the way cryptics made your mind jump sideways, the lovely puns that developed. Best of all I liked the way they revealed the mind that created them. As soon as you understood the way the crossword maker's mind worked, the answers were easy. The ones I did regularly were devised by someone with a great sense of humour and an avid interest in cricket. I wondered what he would have done with Terminal Illness and whether it was the question or the answer. I doodled on the side of the page.

Thirteen unlucky letters for one down. Mark Bannister: one down. How many more were there to go?

MINERAL STILLNESS
A
R
K
B
A
N
N
I
S
T
E
R

1 (across): Terminal Illness's result (7, 9)
1 (down): Stain the handrail (4, 9)

24

Costas didn't take long. A pat on the head and a bottle of cough mixture would fix his troubles.

'Claudia Valentine?' said Dr Mackintosh, looking at the only unfamiliar face in the waiting room. I put the *New Idea* back in the rack and entered the inner sanctum.

Dr Mackintosh sat with pen ready to fill in the blank card that had my name on top, a little weary now after a lifetime of looking at tonsils and listening to hearts.

'I haven't come as a patient, I'm an insurance investigator. I have a few routine questions I'd like to ask about one of your patients: Mark Bannister.'

He sighed. 'Ah yes, poor Mark. I've known him since he was this high.'

'What exactly was wrong with his heart?'

'Arrhythmia. Result of a malformed heart.'

'A what?'

'Arrhythmia,' he said, shifting in his chair and unbuttoning his cardigan. 'Effectively it's an abnormal rhythm of the heartbeat. Do you know how the heart works?'

In ways unfathomable. 'Ventricles is all I remember from school Biology.'

'Well,' he said drawing a heart on my card, 'the heart is made up of chambers: the atria, or upper chambers here, and the ventricles, or lower chambers. Now the upper chambers contract and push blood into the lower ones which pump the blood around the body. This,' he said, scribbling in a circle, 'is the sino-atrial node, which transmits electrical impulses to a mid-point junction here and then on through the ventricles. The sino-atrial node is in fact the natural pacemaker, which controls the rhythmical contractions you know as heartbeats. In Mark's case – I won't bore you with a full medical explanation – there was a gap here which resulted in abnormal rhythm.'

'So he had a pacemaker fitted.'

'Yes. An artificial pacemaker that replicates the function of the natural one.'

'Did you do the operation?'

'No, my dear,' he said with a smile that felt like a pat on the head, 'I'm a GP, and a very old one at that. I'm retiring at the end of this year and having a good long rest.'

'You probably deserve it. I bet you've eased a few aches and pains in your time.' I was looking at the last of the old time doctors, the ones who didn't do Medicine because they got 450+ in the HSC and it was the most prestigious university faculty. Who came when you called, even if it was two o'clock in the morning, who warmed the old stethoscope before listening to your heart, who didn't have baby grand pianos in the waiting room, and who weren't photographed at the races flanked by a drug importer and a High Court judge.

'You can say that again.'

I didn't say it again but I did ask another question. 'Who was Mark's surgeon?'

'Just a minute, I'll get his card,' he said buttoning his cardigan and going to the door. 'The memory's not what it used to be either.'

He came back in with a couple of cards paperclipped together.

'Let's see now ... Dr Prendergast did the first one and ... Dr Villos did the second.'

Villos. I recognised the name. It was in the social pages every second Sunday.

It was also Sally's name. The city was full of coincidences.

'Why did he have two?'

'They don't last forever, they have to be upgraded.'

'How long had he had the second one?'

'Two years.'

'Where was the operation done?'

'At Prince Alfred.'

'I'm sorry to have to ask you this, Dr Mackintosh, but did you know that Mark took heroin?'

The pen dropped and rolled across his drawing of the heart. Dr Mackintosh sighed deeply, shaking his head. 'No. No I didn't. Mark stopped coming to me after that last operation. Oh dear,' he sighed again. 'Why would a boy like that jeopardise his life? Why do young people ...'

'Would someone with a pacemaker endanger his life by taking heroin? Could it interfere with the pacemaker?'

26

'I shouldn't think so, but you'd be better off asking an expert. I'm not an expert in either area. Why do young people do that sort of thing? Why do they find it necessary?'

The question was addressed more to the world outside his cosy office than to me.

I thought of my youth. And of those who hadn't survived it. *Live fast, die young and leave a good-looking corpse.* The cliché had grown old and bitter. Paradise now, even if it was only for a few hours. And once you'd tasted paradise, and knew how easy it was to get more . . . 'The same reason people go to the movies or get drunk. Sometimes reality is . . . insufficient. There's not a human culture on this earth that doesn't have some sort of drug, perhaps it is . . . necessary.'

'Even if it kills you?'

'Is that what you think killed Mark?'

'Miss Valentine, I was ignorant of his addiction before your visit. I'll tell you the same thing I told Mark's sister: if pacemakers allowed us to live forever we'd all have one. People with pacemakers die, the same as people without them. We are not immortal, not even the young.'

Despite the No Smoking signs in the Allergy Clinic, I found Lucy leaning out one of its windows smoking.

'Hey-hey!' she sang, slapping me on the bottom. 'Claudia!'

A cheek-to-cheek hug between Lucy and me was near impossible. She was five foot nothing, thin as a rake and moved like dynamite. At karate she was always the last one chosen as sparring partner.

'Well that's a fine example for your patients. I hope you're not treating anyone for tobacco allergy.'

'Look, it's the end of the day, a packet lasts me a week and I'm blowing it out the window.'

'And where are you ashing?'

'I wait for bald men to pass by and ash on their heads.'

She stubbed the cigarette out on the sole of her shoe and dropped the butt neatly out the window.

27

'Do you know a Dr Villos?'

'Raymond Villos, the heart surgeon? Sure. I catch fleeting glimpses of him along the corridor. He's a busy man. Not a busy doctor but a busy man.'

'Could you arrange a meeting with him? He treated a patient I'm interested in.'

'I could. But you'd have to go to Europe for it.'

'Oh,' I said, deflated.

Lucy was sitting on the desk now, swinging her legs.

'What did he treat him for?'

'He put a pacemaker in him.'

'Here?'

'Yes.'

'Maybe our technician can help. The patient most likely comes here for check-ups.' She hopped off the desk and stood with a hand on one hip. 'He's cute, unattached and heterosexual. He's an angel. Literally.'

I tsked. 'Lucy, do you *have* to do that Thai bar girl routine?'

'What's wrong with Thai bar girls? Do you want to meet him or not?'

'I want to meet him. But not necessarily because he's cute, unattached and heterosexual, OK?'

'I'll page him right away,' she said knowingly.

She tapped her fingernails impatiently on the desk.

'No luck. I'll try another number.' Her fingers skimmed lightly over the numbered buttons, hardly touching.

'Nancy? Doctor Lau here. I'm looking for Steve Angell.'

'Oh. Is he? What time will he be finished? Round about.'

'Uh-huh. Nancy, if you see him beforehand, will you tell him to wait? I've got someone here who's just dying to meet him.'

I grimaced. 'Thanks a lot!' I said when she hung up.

'What's to worry? Lots of people are dying till they meet Steve. He gives them a new lease of life. Don't worry about it, he'll be intrigued. He'll be in theatre another ten minutes, then he's all yours.'

'Are you going to tell me where to find him or am I just going to be drawn magnetically towards him?'

'Out the door, turn right, it's a white building, sixth floor.'

'Thanks a lot, Lucy.' This time I meant it. 'Ah, by the way,' I said, moving towards the door, 'Dr Villos: does he have a daughter?'

'Yes, he does. Only child. Spoilt brat from what I hear.'

'What's her name?'

'Umm,' she clicked her fingers, 'it's on the tip of my tongue: Susie. No, not Susie. Um . . . Sandra, no . . . Oh God, I should know it.' Lucy was nearly dancing to the tune of her singsong voice, 'Sally, yes, that's it. Sally.'

Steve Angell may have been unattached and heterosexual but he was not cute. He was stunning. As tall as me, if not taller, with eyes like the pools you find beneath waterfalls. It was all I could do to stop myself taking off my clothes and diving in.

I waited till he'd assured an elderly gentleman his pacemaker was good for at least another five years, saw him to the door, then turned and gave me what I took to be his undivided attention. He certainly had mine.

'Private detective, eh?' I saw perfect white teeth and tantalising glimpses of a healthy pink tongue. 'That's the most exciting thing that's happened to me all day.'

And meeting an angel had certainly brightened up my day.

The head told the heart to get back in its box and get on with business.

'Most of it's pretty routine, not like in the movies.'

'Yeah, even doctors look good in the movies.'

'Some doctors look pretty good in reality,' I said too obviously. 'I mean Dr Villos, for example. He seems to lead a pretty exciting life.'

'You want to pick my brains about Dr Villos?'

'About a patient of his actually, an ex-patient: Mark Bannister.'

'Bannister!' He winced, as if I'd reminded him of something he'd rather forget. 'What's your interest in Bannister?' he asked, more composed now, fingering an ear that had once been pierced.

'How he died. Heroin was found in his blood stream, could that interfere with the pacemaker?'

'If you OD, you OD. With or without a pacemaker.'

'They found heroin, but not enough to kill him. Couldn't it speed the heart up and blow the system?'

'Heroin slows the heart down, if anything . . .' I wondered what circuitous route had led him to where he was sitting at this very moment.

'What about the pacemaker itself? Could it have broken down?'

He smiled. 'Pacemakers don't "break down". They're super reliable, they're checked and tested and checked again, before during and after the operation, especially after.'

'When was the last time Mark Bannister had his checked?'

'Bannister, Bannister . . .' he said softly, tapping the computer's keyboard. The screen came to life and filled with print. 'Oh, the 23rd.' Two days before he died.

'Did you check it yourself?'

'No. He did it from home.'

'Did it from home?'

'Yeah, you can do that. Usually it's country patients who live a long way from the hospital, but Mark had a modem and tester at home. That's all you need. The transmitter relays an ECG to the clinic. If it corresponds to the picture we have here, fine. If not, it can be adjusted. All through the phone.'

'Did Mark's need adjusting last time he rang in?'

'No, everything was hunky-dory.'

No, not everything. Terminal. Illness.

'Was there anything . . . special about Mark's pacemaker?'

'It was state of the art, dual chamber.'

'Jewel chamber?' Was that like having a quartz clock ticking away inside you?

I must have looked dumb because for the second time that day a member of the medical profession started drawing me hearts.

'The old pacemakers only connected to the ventricles and produced the same heartbeat whether you were asleep or swimming the English Channel. But of course with the old ones you couldn't do strenuous exercise like that. The dual chamber or responsive pacemaker, by stimulating the upper chambers as well as the lower, approximates the natural rhythms of the heart, so that when you exercise the heart beats faster. Young people like Mark Bannister are particularly suitable recipients for the dual chamber. You can swim the English

32

Channel if you want to and you don't die every time you have sex.'

'I can think of worse ways of dying.'

He leaned back in his chair, stretching out his legs and putting his hands behind his head. 'One of my sisters had a bloke die on her like that. Woke up in the morning and found a smiling corpse lying beside her. He was only 48. Put her off older men for life.'

I smiled. I liked men with sisters. It usually meant they treated women as friends. 'How many sisters do you have?'

'Three. One older and two younger. It was one of the younger ones that gave this guy a good send-off. What about you?'

I laughed. 'Haven't yet managed to kill anyone though I've sometimes noticed a certain comatose condition.'

He grinned with his eyes: 'No, not that: have you any sisters or brothers?'

'No, there's only me.'

'Any husbands or kids?'

'One of the former and two of the latter. And the former is former.'

'Divorced?'

'Isn't everyone? It's history now. My husband remarried: nice country girl, content with what she's got.'

'Do I detect a note of sarcasm?'

'Do you? It was my decision. It wasn't easy at the time, I went through a lot of soul-searching. I wouldn't be surprised if there were a few hard edges, scar tissue, especially with the kids, that was hard, leaving the kids.' I kept my eyes focussed, refusing to look back. 'Gary's a good parent. They have a great life in the country. They spend all the school holidays with me, and some weekends in between.'

'I have a daughter in Germany. I miss her like hell. Miss her growing up. I have one month a year with her. Every year she's that bit older, a different person, and I have to get to know her all over again. She speaks English with a German accent. It's a strange feeling when your kid is foreign.'

Scar tissue, but he was still smiling.

'How did you get into pacemakers?'

'Job ad in the paper. I'd just come back from overseas, I'd done a bit of electronics work in Germany, along with a lot of other things like driving trucks to Afghanistan when you could still drive to Afghanistan. Came back broke, found the job and here I am.'

'So you're not a doctor.'

'I did that study after – how the heart works mainly, the rest of it is electronics.'

'Maybe sometime you could tell me how the heart works. The head, I know all about that, but the heart and its motivations are infinitely intriguing.'

'What about tonight? I have some diagrams at home, they're not quite etchings but they'll do. Perhaps we could discuss them over dinner. I'm a great cook.'

He was looking better all the time. Old enough, tall enough, and wise enough not to try and talk to me in the morning.

'I have to work tonight, but I'm certainly interested in trying your cooking. I never cook any more, I eat pub food.'

'What time will you be finished?'

'It's hard to say. I don't have fixed hours, the job takes as long as it takes.'

'Here's my address in Newtown. Come over when you finish. You look like the kind of woman who'd enjoy a glass of champagne at two o'clock in the morning.'

Picked it in one, angel face.

We looked at each other steadily, for what seemed like hours. If I was going to dive into those liquid pools, he was going to get wet too.

But hang on, Claudia, I thought, you've dived in before and found the waters murky and cold.

'I do. But I like the first glass to be a little bit earlier. I'll ring you. Soon. Maybe before dinner at your place we can have a drink at mine. I live in a pub.'

'Right where the action is, eh?'

'It has its moments.'

I had to drag myself away.

'See you soon.'

'Soon.'

34

I turned.

Then I turned back.

'Steve, when I mentioned Mark's name, you recognised it immediately. Do you remember all your patients so well?'

'I remember Bannister, I nearly killed him. The guy had really sensitive ventricles. I was trying out programs on him to find the most suitable. You pick a program by testing each section of the heart. I tried one particular program and his heart went haywire. If I hadn't put a magnet on his pacemaker he would have died.'

Mark's flat was in a street off Campbell Parade. We swung down the hill overlooking the black expanse of Bondi Beach and the lights twinkling on the foreshores. So pretty and so innocent, the facade of lights covered a multitude of sins and one of those sins was murder.

'There it is,' I said to Otto, pointing out a not too salubrious set of stairs disappearing into the dark between two shops.

We were two blocks away before we found a place to park where the shops finish and the houses begin.

'Typical, isn't it,' I snorted as we got out of the car.

'The walk will do you good,' said Otto flippantly.

'Don't tell *me*,' I countered.

My legs are my best weapon. If I'm close enough I can do a karate kick that knocks them flat. If I'm far enough away I run. That's what they mean in the profession by 'using your legs as a weapon'. And I don't carry a gun like some of my more cowboy colleagues. 'Why don't you, Claudia? Can't fit it in your handbag?' If I don't have one then I can't use it and conversely it can't be used on me. There's more than one way of skinning a cat. There are more women in the profession than you'd think. Hardly any of them carry guns and they manage quite well. Like I say, there's more than one way to skin a cat and most of the time it's not necessary to skin it. People tend to talk more, be more open with a woman, less guarded, less wary. If you can get past the cowboys, being a woman in this job is a distinct advantage. The crims don't discriminate anyway: they'll blow away a woman on their trail as readily as a man.

After the first landing the dark staircase branched off right and left. At the top of the stairs on the right was a door with a metal '4' on it. The key I'd managed to extract from the real estate agent turned in the lock and we entered.

The flat was small but surprisingly luxurious for these surroundings. At the end of the hallway was a bedroom with a kingsize bed in it and a CD sound system. Off the hallway itself was a loungeroom with huge cushions around a glass topped table, a TV and video.

The boy was certainly well-equipped.

Off the kitchen was another room: the room that housed the computer and the telephone. I followed the cord down to the wall socket. A modem was wired into the telephone system. Otto glided to the computer like a zombie summoned by its master. The computer sat there blankly reflecting Otto's face in its screen. Mineral stillness. Not a master, a servant. Innocent, clean-cut plastic. Too much like a child's toy to make life and death decisions. It almost smiled. Not the enigmatic smile of the Mona Lisa but the pretty little blond smile of *The Bad Seed*.

These three rooms, the lounge, kitchen and computer room, were lined with windows, curtains now drawn, that looked out over rooftops and the back windows of an older block of flats. There was washing hanging out on those retractable washing lines you see in apartment blocks in Europe. You could nearly reach out and touch it. And from the back windows of those flats you could see right into this one.

It was neat. Very neat. The wastepaper bin, usually such a wonderful little receptacle of people's lives, was empty. There was, in the flat, hardly any paper at all.

'Hmm,' I murmured loud enough for Otto to hear, 'that's strange. Writers are usually drowned in paper and there doesn't seem to be an awful lot about.'

'Not if he's using electronic media,' answered Otto. 'What surprises me is the complete absence of discs.'

'Hmm. I'd say at a quick glance that someone's been here before us.'

Otto fiddled with the computer while I carefully opened empty drawers.

'How are you going?' I called out.

'The hard disc seems to be empty – unless there's a protect

program blocking my software. And I can't find any of his at all. You would have thought he'd have the decency to leave me a game to play with while you're snooping in his drawers.'

'I don't believe a paranoid writer would have all his eggs in one basket. There must be back-up somewhere, a duplicate.' I was calling out to him from the bathroom, having lifted the lid off the cistern. This did reveal some junkie paraphernalia in a plastic bag, but what else is new?

'No doubt,' Otto replied. 'But not necessarily here. There's a modem. It allows this computer to communicate with others. Perhaps he transferred his files then deleted them.'

'Or perhaps someone simply removed them.' I was in the kitchen now. The cupboard above the sink revealed jam, peanut butter and Vegemite, some canisters containing muesli, dried fruit, nuts and pasta, but no discs. The cupboards below the sink with saucepans and crockery told the same short story.

Back in the computer room I held the curtain aside. Through the gaps in the washing I could see to the flat opposite. There was a venetian blind at the window but behind that the light was on. I wondered if the occupant of the flat had seen anything through the window.

'Want to watch me at work?'

'I thought that's what I was doing now.'

'What I had in mind was a bit of interrogation.'

'You mean with thumbscrews and naked light bulbs? Just as well I'm wearing leather.'

On the other side of the landing was flat number 3. I knocked on the door and waited. A radio was playing faintly in the background but that didn't necessarily mean anyone was home. Some people leave the radio on like others leave the porch light on – as a sign to burglars that the occupants are out. Doors which in my childhood were left open all night for summer breezes to waft through were now bolted, alarmed and connected to a central security guard system. A sign of the times. There weren't any drugs then either apart from aspirins in Coca-Cola.

There was no answer. I knocked harder. Not quite as hard as a police knock but one that could at least be heard above the radio.

Otto was shaking his head. I tried once more. Nothing.

We walked down to the ground floor and went through the same routine with number 2. Same story.

'Doesn't anyone in Bondi ever come home?'

'They're probably all sitting in a cafe eating icecream,' said Otto dryly. 'Which is not such a bad idea.'

It has always struck me as a bit of an anomaly that Germans have such a fetish for icecream. In their cold, cold country there's an icecream parlour on every corner.

I tried my luck at number 1, forgoing the soft knock and launching straight into the hard one. No answer. I tried again.

Otto was elbowing me out onto the street when a light went on. 'OK, I'm coming,' came a voice like 30H grade sandpaper. The door was flung open by a young man with a bullet for a head and a towel round his waist. His legs, the only visible part of him not tattooed, were wet.

'Yeah, what d'you want?' he said, eyeing us suspiciously.

'Just like to ask you a few questions about the flat upstairs,' I ventured in conversational mode.

'You moving in?'

'No, just like to know if you've noticed anyone coming or going from it.'

'You cops?' he sneered.

'Not exactly,' I said showing him my ID.

'Look, I don't have to talk to you people,' he said, jabbing a wet finger in my direction. 'As far as I'm concerned, you can PISS OFF!' The wind from the slamming door nearly blew us into the street, a job that was completed by a sudden burst of mega-decibel heavy metal.

'So much for your charm and winning ways, Claudia. You didn't even get your foot in the door.'

'Why don't you go and buy an icecream?'

'Perhaps I will. Perhaps you'll do better on your own.'

We walked to the corner past the row of parked cars. One of them was the BMW. The driver had his head in a newspaper but I was damned sure he wasn't reading it. It was not a comfortable feeling, being the watched rather than the watcher.

'Otto,' I said quietly, 'either this city is full of coincidences or I'm being followed.'

'Why should you have all the luck? Perhaps he's following *me*.'

'Well, we'll see about that. Go and have your icecream. I'll meet you later. And Otto, don't get into cars with strange men.'

'Only if they offer me sweets.'

I walked round the corner and fused with the darkness of a doorway. Karate had taught me more than just high kicks. Pretty soon someone turned the corner. It looked awfully like the BMW driver. His eyes slid into the darkness and out again without seeing me. He walked on then back down the other side. He didn't look pleased. He stood at the corner finishing his cigarette, stubbed it out, then disappeared. I wondered if he knew the 1958 Daimler parked a couple of blocks away was mine. Despite sporadic rapid eye movements on the way over here I hadn't noticed anyone following me. Maybe it was Mark's flat he was watching. I'd certainly be paying attention on my way home. As no doubt he would. Despite the creepy feeling of knowing I was being watched I couldn't help smiling: I was being tailed. I must have been doing something right.

The night was crisp and in between the sounds of the traffic you could hear the surf dumping its rhythmic load onto the beach. When I got round to the back flats I was confronted with a set of locked glass doors. On the wall was a panel of names with buzzers beside them. My eyes climbed to the names corresponding to the top flats. There was a choice: Lisa and Sharon, or Mr & Mrs E. Levack. I pressed the Levack buzzer.

Almost immediately the name panel crackled. I announced myself. If it crackled up there as much as it did down here they wouldn't be any the wiser. There was silence then the doors clicked.

I stepped onto bile green carpet. It was a bit worn in places but in general looked neater than Mark's block with its scrappy

41

brown vinyl. I wondered where you got this particular shade of green. Not that I wanted any. I wouldn't (hopefully) be seen dead on it. It was just that you never saw it anywhere except in rented premises. I climbed the stairs to the top floor and pressed the chime bell button of the Levack abode. They were expecting me – or expecting someone. There was a spy hole in the door and I stood in front of it smiling as nicely as I could.

The door opened and I was greeted by a sight I had not seen for years – a woman with her hair in rollers. Behind her, in a faded lounge chair with arm protectors, was a man, Mr Levack I presumed, with his nose in the paper. Characters from *Murder, She Wrote* flickered across the TV screen and I plunged straight in: 'Good evening Mrs Levack, I'm Claudia Valentine, private investigator.'

'Oh do come in!' invited Mrs Levack, excited as a schoolgirl. 'Fancy that, I was just watching that show on the television and then in *you* come. What a coincidence!'

Mr Levack wasn't quite so impressed. He didn't look up from his newspaper but he did extend a hand in my direction, a hand that stayed there even after I shook it.

'No, not that. I want to see your card, proof of identity.'

I showed him my ID, which he examined carefully, both sides, eyes volleying between my photographed face and the real one. He handed it back.

'Carry on.' And he went back to reading the paper.

'Do you mind if I look out your window, Mrs Levack?'

'Oh no, go right ahead. Someone following you, dear?'

'No.' I smiled. Not right that moment, anyway.

I looked through the venetian blinds straight into Mark's flat, or it would have been straight in had the curtains not been drawn.

'I'll come straight to the point, Mrs Levack. I'm investigating the death of Mark Bannister, who lived over there in that flat.'

'Oh yes, terrible business, wasn't it? Fancy a young one like that dying of a heart attack.'

'You knew him then, did you?'

'Oh no, dear, we read it in the paper.'

From out of the depths of his newspaper Mr Levack spoke, 'It was as good as if she knew him, the way she kept her eye on him.'

'Well, Eddy, it's just as well someone is keeping an eye out. The way things are nowadays, you could be lying dead in the street and no one would lift a finger to help.' Mr Levack grunted and turned the page. 'Isn't that right, Claudia? You don't mind me calling you by your first name do you, dear?' I smiled to indicate that I didn't. 'What is it you want to know, Claudia?' she asked, sitting upright on the edge of the lounge ready to reveal all.

'Anything, Mrs Levack, anything you think might help us with our enquiries. His habits, whether he had visitors . . .'

'Well,' she started, 'he looked to me like the studious type. Not that he wore glasses or any of that, but he spent a lot of time near the window writing or typing. I couldn't see the typewriter but just by the way he sat I guessed that's what he was doing. Habits: well, he drank a lot of coffee, twelve cups a day.' I mentally raised my eyebrows. If ever I needed an offsider Mrs Levack was the one. Twelve cups a day. She didn't miss a thing. 'And sometimes when he brought the cup back from the kitchen – actually it was more of a mug than a cup – he'd stand by that very window looking out – I suppose he got sick of the studying – and you know sometimes I could have sworn he was looking straight at me.'

'Yeah, but you of course ·was behind the venetian blind so how could he see you? I've told you, Mavis, if you're going to look in people's windows at least let them see you doing it. At least that gives them a fighting chance.'

'Oh Eddy, then they'd think I was a busybody.'

'Well?' sneered Mr Levack triumphantly.

'Well what else have I got to do, you with your head in the paper all day every day. That's just as much a busybody, isn't it, only you read about it, I get it first-hand.'

'Humph!' retorted Mr Levack. 'What I read about in the newspapers is important. How many cups of coffee a person drinks a day isn't important.'

'It is, isn't it, Claudia?'

I wasn't about to be drawn into a domestic. Mrs Levack was

on side and that's where I wanted to keep her. I trod the taut rope, careful not to lean one way or the other.

'It *could* be important, Mrs Levack. At this stage we don't have much to go on so anything you could tell us might be helpful.'

Mr Levack humphed again and noisily turned another page. Unperturbed, I continued: 'Did he have any visitors?'

She thought for a moment. 'Only that girl, really, with the hair like a lion's mane. I don't think she was a very good influence though, because whenever *she* came he'd stop the studying straight away.'

I was amazed how much this woman could see through one window, and a window with curtains to boot.

'Mrs Levack, how can you be so precise about what you saw? Surely through curtains you'd only be able to see vague shadows.'

'She had her binoculars trained on him,' Mr Levack snorted.

'They're *your* binoculars,' Mrs Levack threw back at him. Then to me: 'His racing binoculars. Only he doesn't go to the races any more and if it wasn't for me they'd just hang there gathering dust. Shame to waste them really. If you've got a thing use it, I always say. Anyway,' she said, rubbing her hands down her skirt, 'it wasn't through the curtains, it was straight through the window. The curtains were always open, even at night. He was the fresh air type. In fact the first time they were closed I seen him do it. Not the young man. It was an older one that closed the curtains. I remember thinking at the time, That's strange . . .'

'You're always thinking "that's strange",' said Mr Levack. 'If he hadn't had his first cup of coffee by 9 am in the morning she'd be saying, "That's strange, he usually has it earlier than this".'

Mrs Levack cleared her throat and glared at her husband. 'As I was saying,' she said loudly and emphatically, 'I thought at the time it was the police but he wasn't dressed like the police and Eddy said it was probably those other ones, you know, plainclothes like yourself.'

'Private,' said Mr Levack brusquely. 'She's private.'

For someone feigning disinterest he certainly had a lot to say.

'When was this, Mrs Levack?'

'It was then, it was when he died. I didn't get a good look at the man because he pulled the curtain across, so I only really saw the arm and the glove.'

'So did you see this man before or after Mark Bannister died?'

'Oh, after. It was a Thursday because normally at that time I'd go down and cash the pension cheque. But there was that strike on then and they were late, which was just as well, wasn't it, because otherwise I would of missed it.'

'You don't miss anything,' said Mr Levack.

'Well, it's just as well, isn't it, because otherwise we wouldn't be able to help Miss Valentine in her investigations.' Now that she was on to the big words she became appropriately formal with my name. 'See, the young man came and sat down at the desk and was typing or something. Then he kind of went rigid and stared. Just stared. Then he stood up, well, not properly up, kind of bent. He was most upset,' she said leaning confidentially towards me. 'He was using bad language. I could tell by the way his mouth was moving. That "f" word,' she whispered. 'He put his hand to his heart, then up more, near the shoulder, and sort of thumped it like this.' She acted it out. 'And looked at me. Looked straight at me like he was begging for help. Next thing I knew he disappeared. Just plopped over.

'I was going to ring the ambulance, but then the girl came in . . .'

'What girl?'

'That girl that's always there. She just stood there staring too. Her mouth opening and closing like a goldfish. She went into the bathroom then came back and bent down out of sight. She was probably trying to revive him with smelling salts or something.'

'Gawd, Mavis, smelling salts! No one's used smelling salts since Cocky was an egg. Anyway, that's for fainting, not a bloody heart attack.'

'Well, she was probably trying to help him with pills or something, you know, like those pills Reggie had for his heart.'

'That was for blood pressure, not his heart.'

We'd be on to operations soon if I didn't intervene.

'Ahem. Mrs Levack, what happened after the girl bent down?'

'She stood up again. And she picked up the phone and started to speak, using her hands as well. Then her head jerked round and she ran away. She must have gone to open the door because next thing that plainclothes was there. And he closed the curtains.'

'Did you see or hear anything after that?'

'No dear, we went to bowls then. It was Thursday.'

'Yeah, but we did see that police car, Mavis, on the way home from bowls.' Mr Levack turned to me. 'Had the devil's own job trying to tear her away from the window to go to bowls in the first place.'

'Well, we should of stayed shouldn't we? I might have been able to solve the mystery, mightn't I?'

'Look, Mavis, there was no mystery. He just died of a heart attack. "No suspicious circumstances", that's what the papers said.'

'You can't believe everything you read in the papers, Eddy.'

'Thank you very much, Mrs Levack, you've been most helpful.'

They were still arguing about it as I showed myself out.

Back down the bile green stairs I went but I wasn't thinking about the colour of the carpet.

I was thinking about the girl and the man in the driving gloves.

*T*hey will want to know the beginnings, the child that makes the man.

The teacher introduces a refugee to the class, a child from a refugee camp where children suffer from malnutrition. She writes 'refugee' on the blackboard carving it up into parts with coloured chalk. The room is a sea of straw coloured hair with blue island eyes – Aryan children whose fathers have just won the war. They look at me curiously, like a caged animal at the zoo. I hear the word 'scarecrow' and a ripple of laughter pass across the sea. The teacher makes me take my hands out of my pockets and stand up straight. She puts her hand on my shoulder, a heavy hand that prevents escape, and tells the children I am a refugee. The Nazis killed all my family so now Australia is my new home and the children must make me feel welcome. She asks who wants to sit next to me. No one puts up their hand, not even the fat boy with glasses who sits alone.

At playtime six of the boys attack me and make fun of my clothes. In the weeks that follow I seek out the quiet solitary moments of each of those boys and one by one show them my knife. Hold it so close to their eyes they cannot even blink. I will not be the sickly masterpiece hiding in the shadows of an alien land. I have stepped off that ship of fools and waved them goodbye forever.

I was a good pupil. I learned my lessons well. In Poland I was top of my class, astounding the bearded teachers in black coats by having the answer to mathematical problems as soon as they had posed them. In this new land I was 'put back' because I could not express the many things I knew in the new land's language. And of course, my schooling had been interrupted by the history being created in Europe. Instead of childhood I had history. I see the child in the clichéd images of many lost childhoods. The snake-black boots getting closer and closer, the child in a loft smelling of putrid hay, the flashing torches, the black shiny boots encrusted with the

47

mud of our land. The child's mother never daring to look towards the loft, wrapping around the child a cloak of invisibility, the cord rupturing in blood then unravelling like a whimper as the grey soldiers close ranks behind her. Then the long nights the colour of terror, the beds of crisp autumn leaves in the shell-shocked woods, the acid taste of wood sorrel, the stench of fear spurting from the veins of rabbits, the throb of still warm meat.

I went west, chasing the thin, pale, retreating sun. An uncle in France I never found, black-market butter, cigarettes. Using my mother's cloak of invisibility to barter with men in back alleys, lost children like myself.

I learned the geography of my new country. The highest mountain was Mt Kosciusko. The teacher pronounced it 'cozzioscoe' and it stayed in the spelling list for weeks. She did not tell them about Tadeusz Kosciuszko, the freedom fighter, who also went to a new land, America, and helped that country win its independence. How he came back a hero to a Poland again belittled by Russians, Prussians and Austrians taking yet another helping. Who developed a theory of guerrilla tactics. Know your terrain, fight with what you've got, slip through the interstices of the organised ranks.

Nor did she tell the children about Strzelecki, who did deals with the governor to keep that lone Polish pinnacle in a range full of English names. The price was his discovery of gold and a shut mouth.

In this new land I would also trade gold for a mountain with my name on it. I would also be a man who could persuade governors to do my bidding.

The BMW had a home in Bronte and was registered in the name of a Mr Arthur O'Toole. It was early morning as I drove to the address looking in the rear vision mirror all the way. No BMWs as far as the eye could see. Maybe, like the smart little pig of that famous porcine trio, I was up too early for the wolf to catch me.

But not early enough to catch Sally Villos. The phone had rung and rung till it had rung out.

I knocked on the door of a liver bricked semi. Several times and hard.

Eventually the door opened a crack and the oldest woman in the world appeared though all I could see was an eye, a tiny blue lake in a desert of wrinkled dunes.

'What do you want?' she wavered suspiciously.

'I'd like to see Mr O'Toole,' I said brightly.

'You one of them Jehovah Witnesses?'

'No, no, it's . . .' It must have been quite a relief for her to know I wasn't trying to sell her shares in Paradise on Earth because before I even had a chance to finish the sentence she said:

'Come in. And don't let the cats out.'

I wished I could have said the same to her about the smell. Ranging round inside the house were dozens of cats: white ones, tabbies, big black monsters and a few mangy ones of dubious parentage.

'Is Mr O'Toole in?'

'Sit down.'

I looked for a place to sit that wasn't covered in cat fur but there wasn't any. Just as well I was wearing jeans and not the black skirt I'd toyed with this morning. At least the denim was some protection against the claws but it didn't stop seven cats simultaneously leaping into my lap. When I had gently but firmly

49

removed the successful ones I looked down to find the heel of my shoe in a crusty saucer of milk.

'What would you be wanting Mr O'Toole for?' she asked, looking out through those tiny peepholes.

'It's in relation to his car, the BMW.'

'I don't know nothing about BNW. Our numberplate started AJC. I always remember it, Arthur always used to say Australian Jockey Club. But we haven't had a car since Arthur passed away. That was a Hillman – brown, no, it was green, more like khaki . . .'

'You say Mr O'Toole has passed away?' She didn't exactly look like she was grieving.

'Yairs. Let me see now, it must be getting on for twenty years, yes, twenty years this October. It was the Labour Day weekend.'

'Do you have any family?'

'Not so's you notice,' she said, tight-lipped. 'There's only Ronny but I'm as good as dead to him. He never comes to see me, I don't even know if he's alive or dead. You young ones don't know what it's like to be on your own.'

I refrained from reminding her that the old don't have a monopoly on loneliness.

'Still, I'm not complaining, I've got me cats. I've got me work cut out with them, I give 'em a good home. I don't understand how some people just let their cats roam around the streets. I bring 'em in and give 'em a good home. That's where all me pension money goes, in looking after them cats.

'Will you have a cup of tea, dear?'

'No thanks, I'm in a hurry.'

'You young folk are always in a hurry,' she said, managing a smile.

Things didn't look very hopeful in the BMW line.

I looked around the room. Apart from the live cats there were ornaments of cats and on the mantelpiece photos of cats. And people. Dour-faced sepia men and women in gilt frames and a couple of more recent ones: recent for Mrs O'Toole anyway.

I extricated my shoe from the saucer of milk and walked over to have a closer look.

'That your husband?'

50

'Yairs. Looks nice in his uniform, doesn't he?'

'Yes, he does.' I wandered along the mantelpiece a little. 'What about this one, the one of the boxer?'

'That's young Ronny. Not much brains, our Ronny, but very good at the boxing.'

I studied young Ronny carefully. Stocky, curly brown hair – 30 years later he was the man I'd seen on the street corner in Bondi. The man Mrs Levack had seen in Mark's flat?

'Where does Ronny live?'

She shook her head. 'Like I said, could be dead for all I know. Haven't seen him for years, not even Christmas. Doesn't even phone or send me a card . . .'

I hoped she wouldn't think me unkind if I left before the loneliness started.

'Thanks for your time, Mrs O'Toole. I must be going.'

'Sure you won't have a cup of tea? I'm all by meself here, don't get much company.'

Apart from 500 cats.

'No, perhaps some other time. Thank you, goodbye.'

I cleared my lungs of cats and breathed in the hot sharp breath of Sydney. Too hot, too sharp. Up the other end of the street, ominous as a dreadnought, was a navy blue BMW.

I had that insidious feeling Mark must have felt if ever he'd looked up and caught Mrs Levack spying on him through the window – the sort of feeling you get when you look up just in time to see the edge of a curtain fall back into place. The sort of feeling you get when you see the car that wasn't following you pull into the street where you're parked.

My brain was making up stories the rest of me refused to believe. So it's a coincidence. So it's not the same car. So he's decided to visit his mother after all these years.

I walked right past the Daimler and examined the bottom of my shoe for dog shit, a habit I'd brought with me from Balmain. There wasn't any but that didn't stop me going through the motions of wiping it off.

The BMW drove right past. I kept wiping, intent on my task. I couldn't see the driver but the numberplate definitely checked out.

It disappeared round the corner and I followed.

But the streets of Bronte were suddenly devoid of BMWs.

I drove to Bondi, parked across the road from Mark's flat and waited. Waited for the BMW and an explanation of its out-of-nowhere appearances.

I went into a cake shop in Campbell Parade and ordered iced coffee and apricot slice. The coffee was strong, cold and bitter, and did to my insides what the sea did to the outside. Behind me, down a long row of tables voices murmured – Polish, judging by the sounds of schussing which laced the conversation. Probably two mothers talking about their sons. I wondered whether the sons drove BMWs and hung around in crematoriums. Wondered how long it would take for mine to turn up. For a city of nearly five million people Sydney is a very small place, and getting smaller all the time. There must have been a million cars in Sydney but I kept seeing the same one. The atmosphere wasn't yet claustrophobic, but if the circuit got much smaller I'd be gasping for air.

Across the road the sea and sky were hazy blue. It was still early and in any case the shop was air-conditioned, but the day was going to be hot and heavy. Officially it was autumn but the summer lingered on. Not that Sydney took a blind bit of notice of the seasons. Variable, she blew hot and cold like a moody child. Once, in a movie, I heard California described as a beautiful dancing lady, high on heroin, enchanting like the drug, who doesn't know she's dying till you show her the marks. Sydney was like that: not so high, not so dying, only sick sometimes. Terminal illness. Transformed eventually into mineral stillness. She'd been a very sickly child, poxy and plague-ridden. But she'd grown strong, like a mushroom on a dung heap. Like an exotic mushroom I'd seen once at Gary's. A beautiful crimson fungus had sprung out of the ground like a spider flower. But in its centre was a dark foetid substance that smelled exactly like human excrement.

Three young Japanese girls came down the esplanade in knee

length shorts, flitting like bulbuls from window to window: cake shops, icecream shops, fish and chip shops, though the signs said 'patisserie', 'gelato bar', 'seafood mart'. Doors which never closed invited joggers, swimmers and tourists to come in and enjoy themselves. Indulge, I'm yours for only a few dollars – it's only money – taste my wares, sit in the sun in your reflective glasses and take it all in through the pores. Bondi Beach, no need for brochures, the place is its own publicity.

It is only money.

Everything has a price.

Too seedy to be St Tropez, too seedy, too slack, too egalitarian.

C ars sat in the sun silently absorbing the heat, reminding me of childhood summers. Days at the beach and before you went home all the doors of the car would be flung open and the heat that rushed out nearly knocked you over. After ten minutes the car would be aerated enough to get into but even then you had to sit on a towel, crusty with salt, so your sunburn didn't stick to the seat. Then you would drive home. West. Eyes squinting in the harsh light of the setting summer sun.

The car was not in the parking area. Outside the Pavilion were three or four coaches with bevies of schoolboys milling round eating icecreams. A whistle blew and lemming-like they rejoined their coaches.

People bathed between the flags and up one end of the beach was a small group of boardriders. Blue awnings and arches characterised the apartment blocks overlooking the beach. At the south end, where the boardriders were, was Bondi Towers, terraced in mediterranean tiles and 'landscaped'. At the north end was the wide brown sea of sewers.

I had scanned the whole beachfront and found not a trace of my ubiquitous shadow.

But I remembered something else: Robbie. And the 'address' he'd given me: Bondi Beach. Any day the surf's up.

Today the surf was 'up'.

I walked towards a group of guys sitting on their boards in the sand. They looked at me like I was a tourist.

'Hi. Is Robbie down today?'

'Robbie who?'

'Robbie Macmillan. He surfs down here.'

'So do lots of people.'

'Blond guy. 'Bout twenty, 23.'

He flipped his hand towards the riders, some coming in, some paddling out: 'Take your pick.'

'Thanks for your help, fellas.'

I walked down to a group of lifesavers doing drill by the edge of the water.

'Excuse me, I'm looking for a guy called Robbie, blond, 'bout twenty, 23.'

'What about one called Lex, dark, 'bout 30?' said a dark guy about 30.

'No, thanks. Smart arses aren't my style.' I turned my back on him and walked away.

'Hey, Claudia! Claudia!' It was Robbie, in the shallows, running towards me, surfboard under his arm and grinning from ear to ear. Young, eager, not yet bitten enough to be shying away. 'How're you going?'

I grinned too. 'Not bad. How's yourself?'

Our eyes were having a conversation all of their own.

'Can we talk?'

'I thought we were.'

We walked further south, towards the rocks. The sea was deep blue now, the colour of a cigarette commercial. The waves heaved and crashed on the edge of the rock platform but we were well away from that, in a hollow wrought by wind and heavy seas.

'I want to talk about Mark.'

'Oh. Is that why you came down here – to talk about Mark?'

I liked Robbie, liked his youthful eagerness. It reminded me of life before the skid marks. Something wafted up from the memory bank, incomplete perhaps, but I held onto what I could of it:

Bliss was it in that dawn to be alive
But to be young was very heaven

I'd wanted the dawn to last forever. It was guys like Robbie who made me think it could. But there'd been enough of them, the young boys, the blond whose name I couldn't remember, to make me realise my dawn and theirs didn't coincide. Next time I got involved it would be with someone who'd also gone through the dark night and was awake enough to see the dawn. Someone like Steve Angell.

'I want to ask you about the heroin.'

He watched a wave roll in and crash against the rocks before he replied. 'How do you know about that?'

'The autopsy.'

'Autopsy? Are you a cop or something?'

'I'm something, a private investigator. And a friend of the family. I went to school with Mark's sister.'

'I don't think Mark's family would want to know about his . . . bad habits.'

'They might not have to.'

Robbie sat with arms dangling over bent knees, looking back now at the beach and the specks of humanity on it. Slowly he started to speak. 'Look, I do a bit of dope now and then but smack . . .' He shook his head, 'As far as I'm concerned it's a one-way street. I've seen more than one mate go that way.'

'Robbie,' I said softly, 'you don't have to justify yourself to me, we're talking about Mark.'

'Yeah, well . . . with him it was . . . manageable. You'd never know to look at him that he was doing smack. He looked healthy, he didn't hang out on street corners.'

'Where did he hang out?'

'Down here . . . At the video arcade . . .'

'Is that where he was getting it from? The video arcade?'

'Maybe. I don't know.'

'Which video arcade?'

He told me. It was one of those arcades down the seedy end of George Street.

'You guys seem a bit old for video arcades.'

He shrugged his shoulders.

'It *was* the video arcade, wasn't it?'

'I don't know. Maybe . . .' I bored holes into him with my eyes.

'OK, OK,' he said after an interminable silence. 'I know other guys scored down there. I don't know for sure, Claudia, I'm only guessing. Don't quote me. OK?'

'I won't quote you,' I smiled. 'Look, I've got to go. Here's my phone number.'

'In case I hear anything about Mark?' he said cynically.

'In case you want a drink sometime. I believe it's my shout.'

The eyes came back, and the grin. 'I got quite a thirst,' he said, ready for anything.

I grinned back ruefully, too chicken to tell him I'd drunk that fountain dry.

It was there. In Campbell Parade. The sight of it pushed my stomach down to my ankles and started my palms sweating. The esplanade metamorphosed into a Kafka novel: smiles on innocent passers-by became derisive and mocking, dogs became wolves ready to attack on a silent signal. All the windows had eyes and they were all looking at me.

I breathed into my abdomen and gathered force. Gradually the heartbeat came back to normal and the rush subsided. The wolves were back to dogs and nobody was looking.

The dashboard of the BMW was like the cockpit of a super-sonic jet, complete with phone and a computer screen. I would have liked to break into it but if I even as much as breathed on it alarms would go off everywhere. I scanned the beach for ex-boxers in leather jackets. The beach was nearly empty now, even Robbie was gone.

I drove into town with the sun blaring through the windscreen like my childhood summers. Near Taylor Square I stopped to buy a paper. 'Shake-Up in Sydney's Crime World' said the headline. When I got back to the Daimler the BMW was waiting in a No Standing zone. The driver had his head in a newspaper. Probably reading the death notices. I slid out into the traffic. The BMW didn't move. Even when I was through the lights it still hadn't moved.

I drove down Liverpool Street and up Kent with eyes in the back of my head. There was no sign of him. Miraculously in Kent Street I found a free parking meter, pushed a coin into the slot then went and stood by the pedestrian crossing. I waited. I was in a relatively quiet part of town verging on the Rocks where a few years before a hitman in a red Mercedes had gunned down a gangland punk outside a preschool. He'd been visiting his mother.

He came. Slowed down at the crossing and I got a good look at him. He had the heavy look of a cop or someone else who ate too much meat. A rugged head, not too bad for an ex-boxer, that went straight into the expensive-looking leather jacket. No neck was visible though he wasn't at that moment sticking it out. I was the one sticking my neck out. He looked at me too, like I was any girl in the street, and drove on. I waited. He didn't show.

I got back in the Daimler and joined the traffic going over the Bridge. The gaudy face of Luna Park loomed up on the other side. Luna Park: Just For Fun. An amusement park with a plaster grin, its painted lips the entrance to a labyrinth of company titles in which the real owner hid. I turned left into Milsons Point and parked the car in a side street. Ten minutes later the BMW came into view. I got out of the Daimler and walked towards the station. I stood on the platform and waited. He didn't show. I let two city-bound trains go by – just to be sure.

Now I knew. It was not me he was following. It was the car.

O ffice workers gushed through the conduits of Wynyard Station on their way home from work. I pushed against the tide and finally came out to Wynyard Park. At lunchtime on sunny days it was sprinkled with sandwich eaters and, following their trail, the deroes who went through bins. Now it was virtually deserted.

When I finally found out the truth about Guy I haunted the deroes' parks looking for recognition. But those eyes had long since glazed over and recognition did not come.

The last customers, or rather 'clients', had gone and Otto was closing up shop.

'Two days in a row, Claudia, you are gracing my humble store with your presence. Can I interest you in some merchandise?'

'No, but you can interest me in some information.'

'What kind of information?'

'Electronic.'

'Oh yes?'

'Yes. You know that guy who's been tailing me? Well, I've got a pretty good eye for that kind of thing but I never actually see this guy following me. He just happens to turn up wherever I go. What I want to know is this: is there a device you can attach to a car so you can follow its route on a screen without actually having the vehicle in direct view?'

'Of course. The police have started using such a device. They attach a transmitter to the subject's vehicle then follow his route on a display screen. It's all very clean and stress-free. They can even do it from the comfort of the police station. All they have to do is watch where the car stops and radio a car in the area to move in if necessary.'

'My tail has a screen in his car.'

'So much the better. No wonder he's always on the spot.'

'What does this transmitter look like?'

'Oh, it can be quite small – no bigger than a pocket calculator.'

'And where's the best place to put it?'

'Anywhere. Anywhere on the car that's not going to get too hot or be subject to electrical interference.'

'Would you recognise it if you saw it?'

'Of course.'

'OK, let's go.'

It was dark by the time we reached Milsons Point. I took the torch out of the Daimler's glove box.

'What are you doing Claudia?'

'You might be able to see in the dark but I can't.'

'Put it away, Claudia, I have something in my hot little hand that always finds its target, even in the dark.'

'You put it away, Otto, you don't know where it's been.'

'That's the trouble,' he moaned. 'It hasn't been anywhere lately.'

He went over the whole body of the Daimler, caressing it with his little gadget, paying particular attention to the smooth round curves of the rear-end.

'Hmm, getting warm,' he said voluptuously.

Then he found it. Under the right-hand rear fender.

'All we have to do is remove it and your tail will disppear.'

'Not yet, Otto, I have a better idea.'

We drove to North Sydney police station, removed the transmitter from the Daimler and whacked it under the door sill of a parked police vehicle.

'There, that should keep the bastard busy for a while.'

The Villos villa in Harbord was a white stucco Spanish style one a seagull would have been proud of.

I'd taken a chance arriving unannounced but I was on this side of the harbour anyway. As for most Sydneysiders, the Bridge, instead of linking the two sides of the harbour, was for me a psychological barrier. Not that Manly was much different to Bondi, syringes were found on both beaches and people got sick from the pollution, but going across the Bridge was like travelling to another country.

Lights were on in the house with the million steps that led up to a grilled security door.

I pressed a white button and heard no sound. But someone else did: the door opened as far as the chain would allow and I heard the high pitched voice of Sally.

'Who is it?'

'Claudia Valentine.'

In a lot of cases just hearing a woman's voice did the trick. Women opened the door to other women because they trusted them; men for a variety of reasons.

'Who?'

'Claudia Valentine. A friend of Mark's family. I met you at the funeral.'

The door opened fully and an unmasked Sally appeared with the look of a beautiful but naughty child. I wondered if she'd been playing with matches. If she had, she'd cleverly disguised the sulphurous smell.

She looked at me cautiously, waiting for me to open service.

'I'd like to talk to you about Mark, you were the person closest to him,' I said softly, trying to get her guard down. 'I work for the family solicitor. There are just a few routine questions the family couldn't answer. Thought you might be able to help.' I wondered when she was going to remember her etiquette and invite me in. I didn't mind doing it in doorways but interiors were so much more revealing. 'Can I come in?'

She stood aside but those eyes never left me.

'Hmm, nice house,' I said as I entered a hallway full of mirrors and waded through mushroom pink carpet to finally arrive at a living room the size of a gymnasium.

She sat on the edge of a lounge chair, obviously knowing the territory and the psychological advantages, because when I leaned back in mine I was almost lying down. I shifted into a position where I could look at her and not the ceiling, while she continued staring at me from under a canopy of eyelashes.

The eyes were the only part of her staying still. The hands were fidgeting with bracelets and the legs were crossing and uncrossing.

'This is a pretty big house for one person. Do you live here by yourself?'

'No . . . yes, at the moment. My parents are away overseas.'

'Oh yes, your father's the famous heart surgeon, isn't he?'

'How did you know that?' she asked with more suspicion than my question warranted.

'Oh, it's no big deal. I read it in the . . .'

'Tequila?' she said, suddenly bouncing up.

'Scotch, if you've got it.'

'I've got it.' She opened a cabinet that held enough liquor to start a duty-free store and poured me a Scotch, splashing a little down the sides. This was my first drink of the day but it wasn't hers.

'No, no ice,' I said as she dug into the ice bucket with silver tongs.

'It's not for you, it's for me,' she said, piling the cubes up in her glass.

'So,' I tried again, 'your father fixes broken hearts.'

She coughed on her drink and winced. 'I wouldn't exactly put it like that,' she said, damning my crassness. 'He's a doctor. A good doctor.'

'I'm sure he is. He was the one who put Mark's pacemaker in, wasn't he?'

She looked at me as if I was trying to undress her against her will. 'Well, what of it? He did a lot of operations like that, on a lot of patients who are alive and grateful to him,' she said defiantly.

The conversation wasn't supposed to go like this. She was supposed to soften and open up. Maybe her grief was taking a strange form.

I slowly sipped the Scotch then tried a different tack. 'It . . . it must be hard for you having your parents away at a time like this.'

She swallowed then said rather grimly, 'I get by.'

She got up suddenly and went to the window. 'I'm doing all right.' Then she turned on her searchlight eyes, scanning my face. 'It's just that. . . that. . . do you know what it's like? It's so . . . so . . . huge.'

She was biting her lip to stop it quivering.

'Sally . . .' I offered.

She was like a child who'd grazed her knee but didn't want to cry in front of the other kids. 'It's OK,' she said in a small voice.

I was beginning to feel uncomfortable. She was standing up, on home ground, while I was trapped in the luxury of her lounge chair. I got up and poured her another drink, which gave me the excuse to stand beside her and softly say: 'You were the one that found the body, weren't you?'

'Yes. And the outfit. He'd just shot up.'

. . . it wasn't the stuff, it was safe. . . heroin in his blood stream but not enough to kill him.

'What about the man?'

Her reflexes were good. She reeled away as if she'd come in contact with a hot stove.

'What man?'

'The man that came into Mark's flat while you were there.'

'How do you know that?'

'Mark had some nosy neighbours. They saw you, then a man wearing driving gloves.'

'Oh,' she said flatly. 'I didn't see who it was. I heard someone at the door and went and hid. I don't know why I did it. I didn't even think about it, I just did it!' Her voice was getting dangerously close to glass-breaking pitch. 'How would you feel?' Her eyes groped at me, trying to pull me down. But as long as she was answering questions I was going to keep on asking them.

'Did you live together?'

'Sort of. I spent a lot of time there.' She wiped her face with the palm of her hand and drew herself up. 'That day I had a modelling session. But the sets didn't arrive so the studio cancelled. I came back to Mark's place and . . . and . . .'

She bit her lip and heaved her chest for the final statement. 'That's it, OK? That's all,' she said, cutting the air with her hands. 'You'd better go now, I have some things to do.'

The eyelashes came down like blinds as she retreated to some inner fortress. I'd lost her. For the moment.

I wrote my number on a piece of paper and handed it to her.

'If things get too rough and you want someone to talk to . . .'

'I've got people to talk to. Thanks.'

She let me out and I walked the million steps back into the real world.

'**C**arol? It's Claudia.'

I knew Carol from university days, a bright girl from a dull background. Most of the kids she grew up with were in trouble by the time they were fifteen. But she'd come a long way from those days. She was an achiever, a detective now, one of the first to have come in with a degree. She was in a tough profession – not only did she have to be equal to the men in it, she had to be better. And she was. She was straight and to the point. I liked her a lot.

She asked me if I was ringing for business or for pleasure. She knew me well.

'Pleasure. Thought you might like a drink, at my place.'

She was coming over to Balmain the following evening. To look at real estate.

'Yeah? An investment or to live in?' . . . 'Well, you'll pay through the nose for harbour views in Balmain. What time will you be finished?' . . . 'Good, let's meet at eight. At the pub. We can have dinner if you like. My shout.'

Carol graciously accepted.

'Oh, and Carol, I wonder if you could do something for me. Nothing serious, just routine insurance. Young guy by the name of Mark Bannister. Died of a heart attack.'

I gave her a few details to key into the computer.

'His girlfriend Sally Villos found the body. What I was interested in was her statement.'

Carol muttered something about there being no such thing as a free dinner. But we had a history, Carol and I, and favours went both ways.

'Yes, well, I have spoken to her but I don't think it's very pleasant for her to talk about it right now.' . . . 'OK, see you then.'

Today the seasons had collided. The unpredictable child had started off sunny, then clouds had frowned across her forehead. She'd sulked all day and finally burst out in a fitful rain. The brightest thing about the day was that Steve had dropped into it. Had some business to do in Balmain and as he was over this way . . .

We walked through the calm after the storm. Beneath strangler figs, their aerial roots hanging lush like underarm hair. Kookaburras coaxed up their familiar laughter. Kookaburras. Nearly right in the heart of the city.

The sun was setting behind the few remaining clouds, the apricot light intensifying the green of the park to an unnatural degree.

'I spent six months working on Groote Eylandt once,' said Steve as we walked down the aisle of elephantine date palms and bat-filled Moreton Bays. 'It was Christmas, we'd just finished up for the season and a bloke had arrived up with some acid. It was my first and only time.'

We were now right down to where the park jutted out into the harbour. Across from us was Cockatoo Island with its grey metallic buildings and cranes, its ammunition dumps like stepping stones in a watery duplicate of sunset. Despite the DOGS PROHIBITED sign, dogs cavorted in the park, as animals do after bad weather, whilst owners pretending not to belong to them looked at the ever changing view.

'We dropped it down on the beach, 'bout eleven o'clock at night. We sat looking at the sky like three wise monkeys. There were these amazing orange swirls, the sky was literally dancing, like some Chinese New Year dragon flashing light at each articulation. And the most amazing thing about it was the three of us all saw the same thing.'

In America I'd heard enough trip stories to last me a lifetime.

But coming from Steve it was like hearing it for the first time. Love, sweet love, the world as new as a baby. To the east, behind the Harbour Bridge and the city outline, dark blue night infiltrated the grey. We turned our backs on it and looked towards the setting sun, at the bright boats that never left their moorings, an orchestra of ropes dinging against aluminium masts like Japanese chimes. I tucked windblown strands of hair behind my ears, a futile gesture, but it gave me something to do: unconscious body language telling him I was all ears.

The story, like the Chinese dragon, had a coda.

'We slept out on the beach that night and the next morning when we got back into town we heard the news. Darwin had been hit. What we'd been looking at was the tail end of cyclone Tracy.'

I let out a whistle that was quickly eaten by the wind.

He laughed. 'On the beach we thought what good acid it was but the next day we found out from some other blokes it wasn't acid at all. The things you do to yourself when you're young. Travelling to places to slog your guts out, then blowing your money and your mind on drugs of one kind or another. Look at me now: same job for the last five years, nine to five almost, home owner and even a landlord!'

'What's she like, your flatmate?'

'Amanda? She's quiet, doesn't make waves. I go for weeks without seeing her sometimes. She works nights. One of those cafes in Glebe Point Road. And,' he said, sticking his hands in his pockets and hunching up his shoulders, 'I think during the day she puts in the odd hour at Sydney College of the Arts.'

'She'd know Sally Villos then.'

'Why?'

'She goes there.'

'Still? I thought she'd become some hotshot model. Anyway, I don't think she and Amanda move in the same circles. Sally's a beautiful rich, spoilt kid who doesn't know what life is about because everything is handed to her on a platter. Probably be in one of those high class health farms by the time she's thirty, drying out.'

Under the trees it was dark now, though the sky was still

straining out the odd line of colour. We were over by the pool, its old timber walls and grandstands embracing a little section of the harbour that people actually swam in. As long as you didn't look too closely at the floating thing that could have been anything from a plastic bag to a jellyfish, or put your feet on the bottom, it was OK.

'I love this park,' I said as we passed under the old peppercorn tree that branched out generously from the side of the cliff. 'I come down here every morning, well, most mornings, at dawn to do a bit of breathing. Same park, same view, but every day it's different.'

'I'm rather partial to sunrises myself. Pity they're on so early. They'd be much better at a more civilised hour, like lunchtime. But then I suppose all you Balmain people are up at dawn, jogging or walking your designer dogs. There seems to be a lot of them about judging by the evidence.'

'Don't knock it. Council elections are lost and won on dog shit. We even have a contingent of concerned citizens who go around picking it up.'

The city was lit up now, in defiance of the night.

'What time is it?'

'Five to eight.'

'Already? I'd better start moving. Carol is extremely punctual. One minute past the appointed hour she starts tapping her foot and looking at her Swatch.'

'Claudia, that offer of champagne – it still holds. Any night you like.'

'Keep the glasses chilled.'

U p the street ahead of me a woman was leaning into a car. As the motor started she stood back and started walking. It was Carol. I caught up with her.

'You look rather windswept. What exciting things have you been up to?'

'Hang gliding. How did the house hunting go?'

'Not bad. You can actually see the harbour from upstairs.

It needs a few things doing to it but Noni can take care of that. She's making more money as a carpenter than she ever did lecturing. And what we can't do ourselves she'll get one of her mates to do.'

Connections. Everyone in Sydney had mates. Beneath the surface of fair prices and justice for all, business went on.

'Aren't you coming in?' she said when we got to the pub.

'Yes, but I'm going upstairs first. I've got to do something with my hair before it drives me crazy.'

'Does your barperson make a good dry martini?'

'Best this side of the International Dateline. Tell him to put it on my bill.'

She was sitting with her legs twined round the legs of a bar stool about to pop the olive into her mouth when I walked in.

'The table's ready if you want to eat right away.'

'Let's go,' she said, sliding off the stool.

The choices we had made in our lives had blown us apart and drawn us together again. At university we'd done some pretty mad stuff. Like everyone else in the mid seventies we were going to change the world. Blow it up. When Carol got recruited everything changed. She was going to chip away at the structure rather than blow it up. Become the first female Commissioner of Police and change the world that way. But nothing had changed.

She became the career woman and I started getting bogged down in dirty nappies. I didn't really get in touch with her again till I came back from the States, ironically now in the same business.

'How was the martini?'

'Dry. So dry I had to prise it out of the glass.'

Stella heard us and started giggling under her breath. Then she remembered she was the waitress and handed us a menu.

'I'll have the trout with truffle sauce,' said Carol when Stella came back.

'Sirloin for me, Stella. Rare.'

'Side salad?'

'Yes,' we chorused. Then rather too quickly, as if to move away a little, Carol said, 'And a bottle of Chardonnay.'

'Drinks at the bar,' said Stella, turning on her heels.

'Pretty girl, pity about the manners.'

'She's a pretty man as well. Does drag shows in Oxford Street Friday and Saturday nights. Waitressing is a bit of a comedown for her. She only does it to make ends meet, so to speak.'

'Your sense of humour hasn't improved over the years, Claudia.'

'At least I've still got one.'

Despite her 'manners', Stella, when she wanted to, made an art form out of waitressing. She glided the plates in front of us as if they were air. She also had a bottle of Chardonnay, chilled. She poured the taste portion into Carol's glass. Carol nodded then Stella filled both our glasses.

'How's the fish?'

'Nice,' said Carol, swallowing, 'compliments to the chef.'

'How did you go with Sally Villos?'

'Drew a blank.'

'What?'

'Look, a guy dies of a heart attack, it happens every day. They may have asked her a few questions but there's nothing on file. What's the big deal?' Then her tone changed. 'Unless of course this is more than routine insurance you're doing.'

'Well, there was something else. There was heroin in the bloodstream.'

'But that's not what he died of. I did go as far as the autopsy report. And I know about the pacemaker,' she said, dabbing the corners of her mouth. 'Any more questions?'

No suspicious circumstances surrounding the death.

If Sally was as tight with the cops as she had been with me they wouldn't have discovered a thing. I wondered if she'd told them about the man. But I couldn't ask Carol. Not yet. Not till a few more of the pieces had come together. The whole thing was too embryonic to have a miscarriage of justice at this early stage.

*T*here is a question that the innocent ask. They burn with curiosity but finally inflamed they ask. In their world of Bankcards and Sunday lawn mowing they don't often meet a man like me. I look like them. White. Then the thread unravels and I flash them colours of my life. And they, in their curiosity, reveal flashes of theirs. Even a man who believes he is white to the core has colours. The gauche green they hide, the cowardly yellow, the red they spurt forth in anger, the ever present darkness they would rather forget. But it flaps at their shoulders and finally settles there, hunching its scrawny neck in ruffled feathers sticky with blood. Sometimes they put their morality in a box and take out single fibres: 'But you know this man, you've followed him for weeks, you know his habits, you've heard his voice. What do you feel when . . . ?' Nothing. I feel nothing. It is like starting the car in the morning, you have to do it, it is part of the routine.

You can't be in business and have an ordinary man's conscience.

Murders are not committed in hot-blooded passion the way a man might kill his wife. They are planned and carefully executed. The actual act is the smallest part of the operation. A mere manifestation, end product, of the thought that made the plan. A plan that seeks out the solitary, vulnerable moments. Off-duty moments.

In the early days I planned and executed. It was my finger on the trigger. Now I plan and it is someone else's finger on the trigger.

Seek out the solitary moments. Even in a crowd a man can be solitary: unguarded and off-guard.

Assassination on the Rocks. Know your target, know how he thinks, know his habits. Pre-empt him. Lucky (or Unlucky as he's since become known) visited his mother on Wednesdays. You'd think in his line of work he'd be more cautious. But Lucky was lucky for too long. Started to think he was immortal. Untouchable. Not only was he living as if he was, he was thinking

71

as if he was. Made the fatal mistake of believing his own publicity. Never lose sight of the man behind the image because while the image rides on the crest in a bulletproof vest it is the flesh and blood man that is fallible. Shards of flesh and blood in the street are the dying proof.

Lucky Nolan had been in the game a long time. Long enough to get greedy for more. To slice off a bit of the cake he wasn't entitled to. The percentages weren't right. We had an interview and he didn't come up with all the answers.

Family visits are men's solitary moments. They slip out of work clothes and become once again new-born babes. Tangled in the sticky threads of love they falter.

The kindergarten across the road might prove a problem. Choose a rainy Wednesday when the children are inside. A rainy day is good. Windscreens are misted and shapes are vague. He would be busy putting up an umbrella ... waiting for a break to run for it. It would be no trouble picking out his flashy car. Outside the kindergarten. Opposite his mother's house. Do it after. When he's full of tea and scones and mother's milk.

A door opens, a man comes out. No umbrella but he holds a newspaper over his head. He starts to walk across the road. Briskly. Time it for the rain. As he puts the key in the car door the red Mercedes draws level and delivers him a message that blows his brains out.

parked the rented LTD, donned a blond wig, and a pair of dark glasses, and walked round into the video arcade. I could have been wearing a gorilla suit and the teenage boys staring fixedly at their machines would never have noticed.

A gigantic Maori stood at the door affecting nonchalance while his eyes slid all over the place. I bought some tokens from a woman in a glass box and looked for a free machine. There was one down the back. Galaga. Also down the back were two doors. Locked. I imagined someone behind those doors looking at a screen that scanned not only the arcade but the whole city. Someone who knew my face beneath the wig and glasses.

It was stiflingly hot in there though no one else seemed to notice. And sterile, despite the bright flickers on the screen and the electronic nursery rhymes coming out of them. The woman in the glass box was reading a magazine, occasionally exchanging cash for tokens.

Five bombers appeared on the bottom of the screen ready to attack a variety of electricoloured opponents that fired out white arrows. These were the ones to avoid, otherwise your bomber exploded and disappeared. Apart from firing rapidly and knocking out the alignment of opponents at the top of the screen, and those that came swirling in from the sides, you gained by taking risks. This was what I was interested in. It involved capture. If you were within range when the blue light beamed down it took your bomber back up behind enemy ranks. But if you timed your capture and moment of escape successfully you won your bomber back and could then fire with two guns. If you didn't time it right you were eliminated from the game.

I sauntered over to the Maori and indicated with a movement of my head that I'd like to talk to him outside. He gave the machines the once-over with his flick-knife eyes then stepped out on the street.

'What's your problem?'

'Oh . . . you know,' I said, twitching and trying to look like I was hanging out.

'No, I don't.'

I drew a deep breath and prepared for capture. 'I want to score.'

'Keep playing, that's the way to score.'

'No, *score*. You know,' I looked furtively up and down the street, 'smack.'

'The only smack you'll get is one on the bum if you keep up this line of enquiry.'

I was standing at the edge of the blue beam and he wasn't going for it. I pulled another fighter out of my sleeve. 'Ronny said I could score here.'

His eyelids came down to a lazy half-mast and he chuckled. 'You've bombed out, lady. Get lost.'

I 'got lost'. Round the block. To the back alley where the car was parked.

I put the accessories back in the car and went into a hamburger restaurant across the road from the arcade. 'Hamburger restaurant' seemed to be a contradiction in terms but the place was definitely restaurant and the food hamburger. What they had in common was that both of them were plastic. You ordered your food by number at the counter, paid for it with the order, then waited. Quick service was something they prided themselves on, but then it didn't take long to put a pre-made, pre-packed hamburger in the microwave.

I took my hamburger to a window seat with a good view of the sleaze of George Street and especially the sleaze of the arcade. I picked up the hamburger and bit into it. The 'bun', the 'meat' and the 'lettuce' all tasted the same. I looked down to make sure I'd actually taken it out of its wrapper because it tasted like it was still in it.

In an attempt to take my mind off the hamburger I thought about why this end of town copped the sleaze while the other end did not. There were brash new buildings here, great cinema complexes, with bright lights winking you in. But other buildings were closed and dead, waiting for the developers' magic to give them a new lease of life, or maybe just a new lease. Here very few suits walked by but up the other end of town – in Macquarie Street that the Premier looked over, the barristers' chambers, the Opera House and Art Gallery – it was nothing but suits. And that was only the women. Up there was the Strand Arcade, camembert and salad greens on rye. Down this end it was hamburger and chips.

History, geography, connections.

People who frequent the other end of town live north and east with splendid harbour views, or in the extravagant real estate of the city itself. Down this end of town is Central Railway, surrounded by industries whose principal product is pollution. Central is the gateway to the west, inland away from the sea that connects us to the rest of the world, away from the chance of escape. Out there are the millions who didn't make it east and north.

But in Sydney money buys status and is the greatest equaliser. Respectable businessmen rub shoulders with bookies, judges, and high ranking police officers. Commissioners are seen in night clubs with well-known crime figures, and I don't mean statistics: crime figures who themselves are 'respectable businessmen'.

These power links were forged in the early days of the colony along with entrepreneurial skills maintained and fostered as the colony grew into the city that is now the crime capital of the South Pacific.

It was a small community where men of power knew each other intimately.

One such man was Macarthur, enshrined, along with his sheep, on the two dollar note. Ironic that his is now the face of legal tender because it was Macarthur who bought up an American ship's entire cargo of rum, then used it as currency. A rum currency indeed. This is not what the history books like to tell us about Macarthur. Macarthur who brought merinos to a land unsuitable for cloven-hoofed animals. Macarthur who introduced the plough to rut the virgin soil. When the ill-fated Bligh arrived to clean up the colony, the colony cleaned up Bligh. When he tried to put an end to the rum currency, Macarthur and his mates from the NSW Corps deposed him and put him under arrest.

The old boys' network had begun.

Whilst musing on this I was steadfastly gazing at the video arcade where the Maori still stood looking up and down the street, looking at his fingernails, looking in at the players hooked up to their machines. One thing insurance investigation had taught me was never take your eye off the target, because the minute you do, something happens. So I didn't miss Ronny O'Toole when he turned up. There was nodding recognition between him and the Maori, a few words exchanged, then O'Toole got back in the BMW and drove around the corner.

I sprinted across the road in time to see him turn into the alley.

The BMW was parked behind a Customs van. O'Toole was leaning against the van smoking a cigarette.

He could have been a politician's bodyguard, the head hardly moving but the eyes looking everywhere, never at the President himself but at places where the bullets might come from.

I stepped silently back into the shadows. In the shaft of light coming from the back entrance of the arcade I could see him clearly.

O'Toole assumed a more businesslike position as shadows loomed in the shaft of light. Out came two heavy men carrying an equally heavy object. A games machine. They loaded it in the back of the van then repeated the operation. Four times. Then they climbed in the back of the van themselves.

O'Toole threw his cigarette on the ground and closed the doors. In the light a thin spectral shadow appeared. A disembodied shadow, for nobody materialised. O'Toole went to the doorway and carried on silent conversation. Then he was handed a bulky envelope which he slid inside the leather jacket.

The door closed and both the light and the shadow disappeared. As O'Toole got in the van I slid into the LTD and watched the van move slowly down the alley and into the system of one-way streets leading onto the Western Distributor.

The traffic was thin at that time of night, the water under Glebe Island Bridge like ink. They crossed the bridge and turned into the container terminal. The van pulled up and a security guard got in.

I parked on the near side of a petrol tanker and climbed over the fence.

Though I passed the container terminal every day this was the first time I'd been in it. It had the irresistible fascination of all waterfronts. The sheer size of it, if nothing else. The few people that you ever saw down there were dwarfed by the huge orange containers arranged neatly in blocks like a miniature city of high-rise buildings; not the jumbled metropolis of Sydney, but a well-ordered geometric version, including the nooks and crannies created by such an arrangement. A great place for hiding, which was exactly what I had in mind. The huge cranes and associated paraphernalia rose out of this city like gods: strong, menacing and all-seeing. I hoped the occupants of the van weren't the same.

I slid behind one of the blocks and watched. O'Toole and the others got out of the van. O'Toole removed the metal customs seal from one particular container. The container was opened and four games machines taken out and swapped. O'Toole then produced from his well-padded pocket another customs seal. As good as new. They all got back in the van and started to drive away. The security guard returned to his post.

All quiet on the western front.

I mentally photographed the position of the container and filed it away for future reference. For the moment I had a more pressing task: to get back to the car without being . . . Oh Christ!

The petrol tanker had disappeared.

But not the car.

My palms started sweating. The dry mouth came next and a strong desire to go to the toilet. Now I understood fully the significance of the expression 'rooted to the spot'.

My eyes were flame-throwers aimed at the car. It lit up but did not burn away. It lit up because the headlights of the van were staring straight at it.

O'Toole and the others leaped out, going for their guns. The security guard was approaching, also with gun in hand. He signalled them to drive on: he'd deal with this little matter. They got back in the van. But O'Toole didn't drive on. It looked like he was making a phone call.

The guard was now doing his duty. I'd never seen someone that size move with such agility. He was back at the container in a flash, prepared to rip it open if necessary. But it would not be necessary: all he had to do was shine his torch into the spaces in between and he'd have me. My hiding place had become a trap. In this miniature city I was up a dead-end street. My only chance was to take him by surprise. If my aim was true I'd kick him in the balls and when he doubled up, slice him in the jugular.

The torchlight came closer, insidious as a shadow. I was lying down on the cold concrete, knees bent and ready, my whole body tight as a spring. When the torchlight came up this alley he wouldn't know what hit him.

Suddenly there was light from another source. And voices. Breath swirled in the smoky light so close I could feel the dampness.

'Boss said leave it.'

'Yeah? Well my job's on the line if I don't sort this out.'

'Your job's on the line already if I make another phone call.'

There was silence. I guessed they were staring each other down.

The guard spoke first. 'Where's the bloody driver of that car, that's what I want to know. What if he saw the whole thing?'

'Relax. Forget it. What do you think that envelope was for? To make you forget. If you can forget you saw the van you can forget you saw the car.'

'How're you going to make the driver forget?'

'It's all taken care of. That's a stolen car – went missing only this afternoon. The owner's a friend of the boss. Funny it turning up like that now, isn't it?'

'Yeah, hilarious.'

I heard the words but I also heard between them. I got the distinct impression that if it was up to O'Toole I'd be dead already.

I felt better and I felt worse. I was being pulled out of the frying pan. But what sort of fire was I being thrown into? Gun fire? Who was my 'friend' who was giving the orders? The spectral shadow at the arcade door?

I had a good idea what was in those containers and it wasn't anything legal. People were killed for less than this. I could hand the matter over to the police but that would mean telling them what I was doing there in the first place. Was my mysterious guardian angel so sure of my silence? Or was he saving me up for something else?

The guard walked to the van with O'Toole and watched them drive off.

While the cat was away I moved swiftly out of my hidey-hole. And realised just how immense this container terminal was. Even if I ran, there would be an eternity of exposure between me and safe cover.

The guard was coming back. Coming closer and closer. I was in a worse position than before and the escape routes didn't look good. There was the road, which was blocked, the harbour, or a moored container vessel lit up like a Christmas tree. A crane overhung it with several flights of metal stairs leading to the top. Someone clambering up those steps would make a noise like the percussionists of the Sydney Symphony Orchestra all playing at once.

I looked around on the ground for something to throw to divert his attention but the place was as clean as a whistle. Not even as much as a lolly wrapper.

I had to brazen it out or run. My legs were good but I wasn't sure they were faster than a speeding bullet.

Now he was onto me. He was holding a torch in one hand and I was pretty sure I knew what he held in the other. My

79

veins filled with adrenalin. Lots of it. I could smell him, the scent of the stalking animal. My vision was so honed I could see not only the light fanning out from the torch but the source of that light. There was only a corner of metal separating us.

One more second. One more centimetre.

Maybe he saw me but it was too late. With one kick both the torch and the gun went flying. The next split-second kick was aimed a little lower, at crutch level. Then rapid punches: head, solar plexus, abdomen. He moaned in a low sort of way, nursing his vitals with one hand and groping for the gun with the other. I kicked it out of reach and brought the side of my palm across his kidneys.

It would have reduced a normal opponent to a screaming heap. But not this one. Instead of nerves he had muscle, and plenty of it. My leg was poised ready to kick him in the back of the head when he rolled over, swung out with one arm and swept my other leg from under me. I'd never seen anyone so fast on their knees and elbows. He had hold of my leg with one hand and the other was coming for my face. I jerked my head up and away and the fist hit concrete. He still had my leg incapacitated and the smashed fist was coming up for another go. I blocked it and went for the solar plexus again. He moaned and went limp but before I had time to extricate my bound leg the bastard bit into it. And held. A good watchdog, trained never to let go. I sliced at the jugular and the bite relaxed long enough for me to swing the leg out of the way and run in the direction of the ship.

All hands were on deck and all hands were waving. There must have been hundreds of them – all big, fat and hairy. with faces you could break bricks on. The guard was also on his feet and coming towards me like a robot with a spanner in the works.

I looked up again at the ship and the sailors. A rope ladder had been extended and they were all urging me onto it. In Russian. I was caught between the devils and the deep blue sea. I took another look at those sailors and opted for the deep blue sea. I felt the oily water slime over me as I dived and when

I came up I saw bullets skipping on the surface of the water like stones. I gulped air till my lungs were so full of it they nearly burst. Then I dived under again, hoping the stinging sensation in my leg was only the salt entering the wound and glad that Australia was a rabies-free country.

'**G**od, what happened to you?'

'Is there a doctor in the house?'

Steve's house was an old terrace, clean and sparse and Japanese-looking inside. I wasn't exactly as presentable as I could have been, but if we were going to go beyond square one, he'd see me like this sooner or later. Besides, after the night I'd just had, I didn't feel like going home and licking my wounds alone.

I wanted to see Steve, wanted to lie in warm water and be soothed.

He put his arm around me and despite the mess I was in, the contact was electric. It flowed from the shoulders to the tips of everything. And out and beyond and back again.

'Can I use your bathroom?'

'Looks like you already have.'

The bathroom had a sunken bath, with lots of tropical greenery growing fecundly around it, and glass doors that opened onto a darkened courtyard. On hot summer nights this would be paradise.

'You want a bath or a shower?'

'Both. Bath first. With Dettol. Then a shower so I don't smell like a hospital.'

'I'm rather partial to the smell of hospitals,' he said, turning the taps on. 'I'll be in the loungeroom. If you want anything just whistle. You know how to whistle, don't you?'

'Not as well as Lauren Bacall but enough to make myself heard.'

When he closed the bathroom door I did whistle.

A low whistle.

The bathroom was filling up with steam and I wondered how much of it I was contributing. I took off my foul boots and black tights, easing them over the purple and red lump that was oozing out of my leg. On the way I discovered a few more bumps and grazes. I tipped up the bottle of Dettol and watched it swirl milkily into the water. Then I stepped in gingerly, waiting for the sting that would cleanse the wound.

There was a knock on the door and before I could answer it opened.

'Thought this might help,' said Steve, handing me a glass of champagne. 'Cheers.' And our glasses clinked.

'How did you get that?' he said, looking at my bite.

'Mad dog. There is a longer story but that can wait till later.'

'Let's have a look at it.' He put his glass down on the timber surrounding the bath and I showed him my leg. 'Hmm,' he murmured professionally, 'contusions and laceration but I think you'll live. Keep a hot pack on it.' He took another sip of champagne and I took a gulp. 'Would you like me to wash your back?'

This time I sipped instead of gulping. It wasn't my back that needed washing, although that was as good a place as any to start. 'You might get wet.'

'I'll take off my clothes.'

'What if your flatmate needs to use the bathroom in the middle of the night?'

'Amanda works nights. She won't be home till about six.'

He'd already started getting undressed, pulling his T-shirt up from the back of the neck like men do and breathing in and unzipping his jeans. This was always a moment of truth for me, the first time I saw the naked body. Sometimes the shape looked all right in clothes but the skin wasn't right, or there were rolls of fat, or too well-developed pectorals that made them look like they had breasts. But if angels had bodies they'd look like this. He was long and graceful, with skin that shone like copper. I took another sip of champagne and looked at the greenery. Things were getting decidedly languid. He stepped down into the bath and I moved my legs aside. The bathwater lulled over the sides but no-one seemed to mind. I didn't give Archimedes a second thought.

'Turn around.'

I turned. He cupped water and dribbled it down my back. Then soap in circles and hands massaging the shoulders, then the vertebrae, all the way down. 'Lean back,' he said.

He poured water on my floating hair. Then shampoo. Then water again to rinse. I closed my eyes and floated on bubbles of champagne, unable to wipe the grin off my face. I felt no pain.

He kissed me on the forehead.

'Hmm.' I was aware of the water level going down a little, and the door softly closing.

I decided I didn't need the shower, stepped out of the bath and dried quickly but tenderly, lightly dabbing the sore spots.

His bathroom cupboard was full of hospital stuff: surgical gloves, creams, elastic bandages and adhesives that didn't tear your hair out when you took them off. No syringes, thank God, or white powder in unmarked jars. There was also the other side of things: the bath oils, herbal preparations and vitamins.

I put some vitamin E cream on the minor bruises and cuts and a thick wad of bandage on the bite and wondered how the security guard was getting on.

'Steve?'

'In the kitchen. Come and give me a hand to take some of this stuff out.'

He looked me up and down, mostly at the area the towel was covering.

'Would you like to slip into something a little more comfortable or would you like to eat naked?'

I'd tried that once before. It was nowhere near as erotic as it sounded: your bum kept sticking to the chair.

'I'll slip into something a little more comfortable.' Like your bed.

'Here, take these,' he said, handing me two plates with perfect bacon and mushroom omelettes, chipped potatoes and watercress salad. 'I'll get you a kimono.'

It was midnight blue with silver things on it that bounced light. I slid into it, and felt the soft caress of silk.

He popped the cork on another Veuve Clicquot: the fumes swirled up and the popping bubbles swirled down into the glasses.

'Where did you get the name Angell?' I asked, digging into the omelette.

'Where does anyone get their name? From my father. My grandfather was Angelo. He anglicised it: not Angles but angels, to quote St Augustine.'

'Do you often quote St Augustine?'

He grinned. I liked his quiet manner and crinkly eyes. 'Only in answer to that particular question.'

'Oh, I see it's not the first time you've been asked.'

'First time I've been asked by a Valentine.'

'Touché.'

He was a neat eater, putting his knife and fork down every three mouthfuls or so. He had a patience and calmness that would either soothe or irritate the hell out of me. I was aware that my plate was empty and nibbled bread to keep time with him. And slowly sipped the widow who must have been some woman to have a champagne named after her.

'What sort of electronics work were you doing in Germany?'

A laugh popped out of him like a jack-in-the-box. 'It's funny a private investigator asking me that because what I was doing was illegal: phone tapping.'

So his wings were tarnished. But it didn't put me off, it made him more interesting. Pure white can be deadly boring.

'Don't worry,' he said. 'I was doing it for the good guys. I was working for the Green Party.'

'And no one heard you cough?'

'The methods are so sophisticated now there's no way of telling if you're being bugged. Not like the old days when you couldn't even breathe. Telecom does it all the time. To check on their operators and ... whoever else may say something interesting. Perhaps I could be of service to you sometime,' he said, inviting me into his eyes.

'Perhaps you could,' I said, inviting him into mine. 'Perhaps you could tell me more about pacemakers now that you are off-duty. Are you sure they're impeccable?'

'Absolutely,' he said, laying his knife and fork side by side and taking up the glass.

'Would an autopsy be able to tell if there was anything wrong with a pacemaker?'

He grinned. 'I bet you were the sort of kid who when your mother said "Don't touch!" you did anyway.' He partook of the widow, pursing his lips together afterwards. 'First, an autopsy examines the flesh-and-blood body only, and second, when the heart dies the pacemaker goes into stand-by mode. A blank screen so to speak.'

'But you said at the hospital Mark's was programmed. How would you know if it was still the right program?'

'By putting it into action. You want me to run a test on it?'

'No, not really. Besides, it's too late now. He was cremated. I doubt they'd give Mark's family a box of ashes with bits of pacemaker in it.'

He put his glass down and looked surprised. 'Didn't you know? When the patient dies the pacemaker doesn't. They're taken out and used again. Particularly if the patient's cremated. The pacemaker would explode. Mark wasn't the first recipient of his pacemaker.'

'What?' My head reeled, making quantum leaps. Technical immortality and human mortality. And when we burn our dead we cut out their hi-tech hearts. Their exploding hearts.

'So while we live and die the manufactured parts go on and on.' Science fiction had become science fact. 'I once read a Jorge Borges story about these talking, thinking metal boxes. They were people who'd had all their bits replaced. They had achieved immortality and all they wanted to do was die. They couldn't: it was a nightmare.'

'If you like reading, have a look at this,' said Steve, placing before me a book entitled *Are Computers Alive?* 'It puts forward the view that computers are the new life form, the latest stage in evolution.'

'That's a bit far-fetched, isn't it? Isn't the ability to reproduce the definition of life?'

'Computers can make other computers.'

'Yes, but they need electricity, and the components, surely.'

'How far do you think organic life would get without air, and sunlight and water?'

'Yes, but they have to be programmed.'

'What makes you think we're not programmed?'

It was starting to sound like the Borges story. 'I won't buy it.'

'That's only because you're set in a human way of thinking, that we are the be-all-and-end-all, that our so-called creations are subservient to us. Maybe we are witnessing the evolution of a new species without really understanding the implications of it. Like the chimps watching *homo erectus* run on two legs across the savannah, holding a stick between his fingers and opposable thumb and chattering away with his freed mouth.'

'Oh God,' I said, sinking.

Steve crinkled his eyes and grinned. 'No, not quite. Look, there's nothing sinister about it as far as the pacemakers are concerned – a new pacemaker costs something in the vicinity of $4000, whereas refurbishing it costs $600. The metal bits are cleaned in a chemical solution and the plastic bits changed. It's a question of money, that's all.'

'That's all it ever is, isn't it?' I said grimly.

'Life's not that tough, is it, Claudia?' His voice soft as down.

The pores opening like flowers to the sun, even after he'd finished speaking and sat with his elbows on his knees, one hand dangling and one holding the glass.

I shifted close to him, put my arms around him and found the soft secret parts round the neck where the curls fell down. Butterflies shimmered madly and 'No,' I murmured, 'no.'

Up here is the postcard view of Sydney. I glide effortlessly along streets, jump from building to building, and finally arrive at the harbour, the brief green parks with the distance-neat Moreton Bay figs. Moreton Bay was a penal settlement, the tree it's named after buttressed and dark, providing shade for the city heat. I soar over tall buildings, columns of glass and concrete, the flat roofs with air conditioning units, some of them dripping Babylonian gardens.

Nothing is ever still in this city, not even the buildings. Whilst one tumbles to the ground another climbs into the sky. Isostasy. Crane drivers in hard yellow hats eat sandwiches, their legs dangling down the concrete canyons. I could reach out and touch them. They do not see me, nor do they know I put them there. Pawns arranged in a pattern. I have always taken a special interest in the development of this city. Its growth and mine are inexorably linked.

When it was nothing but tents and muddy tracks the Governor had wanted 'a healthy city, with sunshine and air'. The streets were to be 200 feet wide, edged with big allotments. But the city grew of its own accord, along the bullock track that was George Street, its tentacles reaching west into a great forbidding land. The governors have always tried to impose a shape on Sydney, a clean ordered mirror image of the upright citizens they purport to be. But the city has a life of its own and grows its own shape. To stand at the top in this city you need to recognise the shape and grow with it. To see the shape of the future, to slip through the interstices and occupy the vacant spaces, to know what will become weeds and end up as dead wood, what will be nurtured and thrive.

Up here I trace out the shape of things and mesh my plans. Then I go down into the streets and execute them. To sketch the mountain, view it from the valley. To sketch the valley, stand on the mountain. To see the shape of the street, stand above the city.

The people in the street never look up. If they raised their eyes just a little they would see the history of the city. Just above the glass facades are older facades. Mouldings, chimneys, gargoyle faces, dates, carved out of stone, the history is visible if you know where to look. The overview does not miss detail: behind the blatant signs are secret hidden things. Beneath the concrete and glass there is a stream. The early colony's only supply of fresh water. Convicts built a bridge across it. It was paid for in rum. This pattern has continued: the currency is no longer rum but derived from the euphoric towers of Asia. The bridge has disappeared but the sign of it remains: Bridge Street. The bridge now has the shape of government buildings, whose dusty basements get damp with the push of water from below. A heavy layer of bitumen and stone to keep the memory of convicts and rum at bay. But these things have a way of seeping through the interstices of the city, the chinks in the armour through which I too seep.

There is more hidden from view: following the course of the stream are the sewers of Sydney, the labyrinthine underbelly, the city of the night.

Incise the tegument with a needle-sharp knife. Expose the viscera, the veins, the roadlike veins, the transport of deadly cargo, the bloodstream of the city's body.

There are more subtle ways to kill than bullets.

Someone had been in my room. Nothing was missing, nothing rearranged, but the smell was there, the smell of intrusion.

I'd come home in a dream, wanting to lie on my bed and dream it all again. We'd slept finally, Steve and I, slept in each other and woken at the same time, like one body, touching and caressing and making love again and sleeping, as if we'd been doing this all our lives. We had watched the dawn spread its colours like some shy elusive bird, watched the city come alive with it. We saw shafts of light as Amanda tiptoed through the house, and pressed silent fingers on each other's lips to seal off any intrusion.

But intrusion was right there in my room and I could smell it.

I went over everything. Opened every drawer, looked in the pages of books, my clothes and lacquer boxes, dragged everything out of cupboards, the fridge, looked in the oven, the phone, the cassette recorder, lifted the carpet, squashed a cockroach looking for bugs.

Then I found it. Out on the balcony, in the innocent mist of lavender leaves. The card that had sweetly said 'To my Valentine' had been replaced by another:

THE LIFE AND CRIMES OF HARRY LAVENDER

Ominous black letters, the same letters as had spelled out TERMINAL ILLNESS.

Whose Valentine was I now? I stared at the clues looking for answers. But there were none. Or too many. Valentine Lavender, the letters slipped anagrammatically, Valentine Lavender Valentine Lavender Lavantine Valender . . . No, no!

I flung the pot of lavender down into the street, watched it smash and the pile of dirt it left on the road. Lavender. Instead of remedying giddiness and faintness it was causing it.

Harry Lavender. Every person living and breathing, and many that were dead, knew the name of that cancerous growth that went by the sweet name of LAVENDER. Lavender owned this city. Had it sewn up. Its life and crimes.

I had a special reason to know it. Lavender had turned my father from a top journalist into a shadow that haunted the parks of the city, quoting headlines that no one believed, sleeping now under the newspapers he used to write.

It was time to plug into the old boys' network.

'Brian Collier please.'

There was a few seconds delay then a male voice said: 'Newsroom.'

'Brian Collier?'

Off-stage I heard: 'Hey, Brian. Phone.'

A few more seconds delay then another voice, a deep voice, the sort of voice you'd be safe with up a dark alley. The voice of Brian Collier.

'It's Claudia Valentine. Guy Valentine's daughter.'

He said that was my tough luck.

'I know.' How many tears I had cried for suffering humanity, for all those whose shortcomings were bigger than themselves and must be borne by others. 'I have to talk to you.'

He said that he was listening.

'Not over the phone. Can I meet you somewhere?'

He started reminiscing about Guy Valentine's kid, remembering the three-year-old who galloped round the house on a hobby-horse. He asked me if I still had the red ringlets.

'Still got the red. Not the ringlets.' I hoped there wasn't going to be much more of this. I felt like an onion, with the tough brown skin peeled off to reveal the layers that made you weep. 'Can I meet you somewhere down there in Ultimo? Buy you a drink maybe?'

I didn't know the Rose and Crown but I would find it.

A NEW FACE ON THE SCENE
By Guy Valentine

It is not every day that an amusement arcade is the scene of celebration. But last Sunday in a certain city arcade the popping of corks replaced the more familiar pops of the shooting galleries and pinball machines. And it looks like a newcomer, let's call him Harry, is the one scoring the points. A war orphan, the story goes that Harry escaped from his native Poland and made his way to France, thence to Australia, bringing with him the family silver. He may not have brought all the cutlery but at least he brought the knives. And his wits. Both of which he has been putting to good use, it seems. It is probably a coincidence that only a week after the slaying of George Gabon, who has suffered so much bad luck lately with a number of fires in his various premises, this celebratory party took place. The owner of the chain of arcades which has been miraculously free of fire made a short speech in honour of Harry, toasting him most warmly, and singling him out as a young man who will 'go far'. Of course we can only guess what the newcomer has done to earn the patronage of such an influential figure in the field. My guess is that the young pup has been blooded.

The clipping, along with the very few others I had gathered on Lavender, was yellowing. For a man who figured so largely in the legends of the city, there was very little about him in print.

Jack was opening up the bar when I went down. 'Did I have any visitors last night?'

'Not that I know of. And you know no one gets past without me seeing them. Were you expecting anyone?'

'No,' I said dryly.

'What happened to your leg?'

'Mad dog.'

Jack was slowly shaking his head and smiling wryly. 'I don't know why you keep doing it, Claudia, I really don't.'

'Pays the rent, Jack.'

We'd had this conversation before. Many times.

The Rose and Crown was a nice pub with lots of dark wood and little bowls of nuts at the bar. I ordered a mineral water and looked around for Brian Collier. All I remembered of him was that he was big. But then when you are three everyone is big.

'Over there,' said the barman indicating a rugged looking man in a tweed jacket sitting at a small table by the window. His body matched his voice.

'Brian Collier?'

He nodded.

I extended my hand in the age-old gesture that showed I was bearing no weapons.

He shook it vigorously. I sat down.

'What are you drinking?'

'Mineral water,' I said sheepishly, indicating the nearly full glass.

'Oh, you're right then. Did you have any trouble finding the pub?'

'Drove straight to it. Parked right outside the door.'

'You were lucky,' he said. 'I've given up bringing my car in. Never find a parking spot.'

The small talk ended and the silence began. It embarrassed Brian Collier and he cleared his throat.

'What was it you wanted to talk to me about?'

'About that article you had in the paper a couple of days ago, about the shake-up in Sydney's gangland. Which of those theories you mentioned do you favour?'

'You sound like a reporter. Are you?'

'Maybe it's in the blood.' I wondered whether the alcohol was in the blood too. I kept an eye on it but there were nights when I let go, nights when there was no tomorrow.

Moderation in all things, including moderation.

'You still haven't answered my question.'

'I know.'

'Ms Valentine, what makes you think I'm going to spill my guts to a perfect stranger?'

'I'm not perfect and I'm not a stranger. Guy . . . my father . . . was a friend of yours.'

'Have you seen Guy lately?'

'I've looked but I haven't seen.'

No recognition in those yellow viscous eyes. It was hardly more than a habit now, looking for my father. Like a sore you picked at, or a tooth you just can't leave alone. Wondering which dero was my father, wondering if he was still alive. First I'd denied him. Couldn't accept that one of those humans in railway stations and on park benches, beards dribbling saliva and pants full of piss, could in any way be related to me. Then I was going to save him, find him and bring him in from the cold. Mina had tried till eventually she had to save herself. Save us both from the darkened room and the fortress of empty bottles that incarcerated him.

'Would you recognise him?'

'Probably not. The last time I saw him I was five.'

'I saw him. A few years ago. Standing in line with the other derelicts outside Social Security in Clarence Street. Not a pretty sight.'

'Did . . . did he recognise you?'

'I spoke his name. He didn't even blink.'

I quietly closed the door on my unblinking father. Too many wraith-like memories to have them come sliding out at a time like this.

'I'm a private investigator. I have a professional interest in your theories.'

'Didn't you read the article?'

'Of course. But that's just the words.'

Collier lit a cigarette and leaned back in his chair. 'I probably won't be telling you anything you don't know already . . .' he said, dragging leisurely on the cigarette.

'. . . My least favourite theory is the Asian connection. I've been watching this game a long time. The Asians stick pretty much to themselves, they've got their own organisation and operate within that. There's a possibility it's blokes up from Melbourne trying to move in on the action up here because, believe me, the action *is* up here. But . . .' he moved his hand from side to side, indicating we were on shaky ground with this one, 'they'd have to have damned good connections in Sydney anyway. It's a bit of an uphill battle trying to move in on a scene when you're not familiar with the geography . . .' I nodded, encouraging. 'No,' he said, finishing off his Scotch and ice, 'my guess is that people are being kicked upstairs. I saw it happen in the sixties and I'm seeing it happen again now. And when I say upstairs, I mean upstairs,' he said, meaning heaven. 'A man can't live forever. They get sick and they die. And sometimes they die without being sick.'

Terminal illness.

'You haven't mentioned the police corruption theory.'

'No,' he stated simply. 'I threw that in because it's topical. There has always been a, let's say, "close bond" in this state between organised crime and the forces of Law and Order. Stands to reason, doesn't it. I'm not denying the enquiries and Royal Commissions have an effect. The effect is the protection gets more expensive and you don't say things over the phone like you used to. But that's not why the crims are shooting each other.'

'Why are they then?'

'Takeover bids. That's what I'd put my money on. Like I say, no one's immortal.'

'Who in particular is not immortal?'

He leaned back and chuckled. I began to wonder which side of the fence he was on but journalists are observers: they sit on the fence and look both ways. Without fear or favour. Collier was more cynical than Guy had been. He'd survived.

'I only get the rumours, and you know what rumours are – a lot of smoke and very little fire. But one of the smoke signals is . . .' he lit yet another cigarette and extinguished the match with a quick flick of the wrist, 'about a gentleman who goes by the name of Harry Lavender. Ah, I see you've heard of him. Rumour is . . . he's dying of cancer.'

Dying of cancer. If Harry Lavender ever did die that is the way he would go. He wouldn't be gunned down, he wouldn't die in jail. It was strangely appropriate. Some sort of poetic justice. His own rot killing him. Terminal illness. The life and crimes ..'. Who was trying to point me to Harry Lavender?

'But that's just a ploy, isn't it? A ploy to stay out of court: cancer, emphysema, pains in the neck, the 'flu . . .'

'Have you noticed Lavender being summonsed lately?'

'I think I need another drink.'

'Another *mineral water*?'

'No.'

Without getting up Collier ordered two Scotches and ice.

'So, they're standing in line like vultures waiting for him to go.'

'Could be his underlings are lining up as possible inheritors of the empire – or could be the empire is about to be carved up by the other princes.'

'What about Ronny O'Toole?'

'What about him?'

'Is he in line for the throne?'

Collier curled his lip. 'Wouldn't say so. He's too dumb and Harry's too smart. You need brains to run an empire. Mind you, he's probably dumb enough to try.

'By the way, where did you get the name Ronny O'Toole from? He hasn't used that name for years.'

'What name is he using?'

'Several. The one for which he's best known is Johnny the Jumper.'

I shuddered involuntarily and tucked my legs under the chair. Everyone did when they found out what Johnny the Jumper's favourite party trick was.

Other henchmen simply shot their victims, or beat them to a pulp. Johnny broke their legs. The kitchen was his favourite spot. He used two chairs. He'd sit them on one chair and tie their legs to the other. Then he'd get up on the kitchen table and jump. Onto their legs.

I felt sick, the sick feeling you get when you hear an urban myth. And sicker. Because this man roamed the streets. Some of the time, it seemed, after ME.

But my legs were still intact. It didn't make me feel better. It made me feel worse. Why *were* they still intact? There'd been plenty of breaking opportunities. And others as well. He could have blown me away at the container terminal . . . he could have blown me away in my sleep. But the worst that had happened to me was being watched. Perhaps even now I was being watched.

'Expecting someone?' asked Collier.

'Why?' I said, jolted back to reality.

'The way your eyes are rolling round the room. Are you in trouble?'

Trouble was swirling all around me, yet somehow I was the centre of it, the eye, the private eye, of the storm. Untouched. That indeed was the trouble.

I laid the card on the table.

'What do you make of this?'

He examined it closely, turned it over and looked at the blank side. 'Looks like the title of a book.'

'A book you've read?'

He laughed. 'No. I'd like to write it, though.'

'I think someone may have beaten you to it. Does it mean anything else to you?'

He shook his head and shrugged his mouth. 'You tell me.' He leant across the table into my intimate zone. 'Where did you get it?'

'It got me. Flew right onto my balcony. And I don't think it was an accidental landing. Does the name Mark Bannister mean anything to you?'

'Yeah . . . yeah. That was that young bloke in Bondi died of a heart attack, wasn't it? It's a worry when people younger than yourself start keeling over: you begin to think you're overdue. And talking about overdue, I'm a patient man but so far you've been doing all the asking and I've been doing all the answering. 'Bout time for a change of chairs, don't you think? What's this Bannister bloke got to do with Harry Lavender?'

'That's what I'm trying to figure out. There's a strong

98

possibility that heart attack wasn't accidental. The guy had a pacemaker . . .'

'I know, that's what made it newsworthy. So nobody's perfect, even medical technicians.'

'Apparently they are. But there's more: he had heroin in his bloodstream.'

'The streets are lined with bodies with heroin in their bloodstream.'

'There's more still. There's that,' I said, throwing my eyes towards the LIFE AND CRIMES, 'and there's this.' I showed him the TERMINAL ILLNESS card. 'And Ronny, Johnny the Jumper, has been following me.'

'He gets his kicks in strange ways.'

'But I haven't been kicked. Just followed.'

I told him about the container terminal.

'Sounds like someone's looking after you.'

'Yeah, but for how long? Someone out there is watching every move I make.'

'You sound just like your father. He thought he was being watched.'

'Well maybe he was!' It had come out too fast. And unexpectedly.

I swallowed, trying to push the rest of it back down.

'Look, you grew up with a story, and the story got bigger and bigger. The Lavender of 30 years ago was just another punk with a knife. A smart punk, an ambitious punk, but he didn't have the clout then. Guy didn't handle it properly. I've been threatened too, but I didn't stay home and drink myself stupid.'

'He threatened to cut Guy's wife and baby. That baby was me, for God's sake! You know what my earliest memory is? Of a knife slicing open the fly screen on the window. You know what that sounds like in the dead of night? *It's insidious, like the creak of a door in a haunted house. There'd been phone calls, and my parents arguing, but after that Guy started staying home. To look after us! But in the end it was us looking after him. Then we lost him. He was still there physically but the mind was off with the fairies. Mina used to hide the bottles at first but he'd go out all night and come*

*home in the morning drunk. One time he'd wet himself, in a
line down his trousers. For a kid to see her father like that?
... Do you know what it's like? Do you? Do you?'* I couldn't
get the noise out of my brain. It was so loud and distorting
people were starting to look.

He put his hand on mine. 'I know,' he said softly. 'Guy
phoned me that night, about the knife. Claudia, your dad
wasn't cut out to be a journo: too romantic, too idealistic. He
was a bloody good writer though.'

'Yeah, he was a good writer: good at writing himself off.
Mina did her best, but in the end she had to save herself.
She left. Maybe she thought that would bring him to his senses
but . . .'

Collier was looking at me with deep brown eyes, the rugged
face soft now as he listened to the story of yet another life.

'Do you know what Mark Bannister was doing? He was
writing a book.'

'The Life and Crimes of Harry Lavender?'

'Possibly.'

'No one would do that while Harry was still alive.'

'Mark Bannister had a computer. With a modem attached.
Now why would a writer need that? You're a journo. What do
you use a modem for?'

'To ring in stories.'

'Do you receive stories as well?'

'I receive information, yes.'

'Do you see what I'm getting at?'

'Oh no, no,' he said, shaking away the realisation. 'Leave it
alone, you don't know what you're up against. Lavender's got
fingers in every pie in the shop. He's got the games arcades
sewn up tight as a bull's arse in fly season. You go through
the company titles, it comes back to Lavender. You look at the
heroin trade, at the man behind the men, it comes back to
Lavender. All the development in the city, the licences granted,
even the legit business, dig deep enough and what do you
turn up? Lavender. And then he's got his own little personal
sideline: computers. Gets the computer to knock him up a
couple of million dollars' pocket money. He knows the way

things are going in this city and he's always one step ahead of the game. You wouldn't get to the end of the first round with Lavender.'

'Been doing all right so far.'

'Are you sure?' he said snidely. 'You think you're running the show? You know how cats play with mice? They tease them a little first, make them think there's a way of escape. They enjoy the hunt, enjoy watching the mouse's feeble attempts at defence. Then when they're tired of playing they move in for the kill. Leave it alone. Lavender's already been given the death sentence. It's just a matter of time.'

'I've got a job to do.'

'What crap! Is your job worth your life?'

'My life is obviously worth something to someone.'

'Yeah, but for how long?'

The question hung in the air like a noose from the gallows.

In a low voice Collier continued, 'What makes you think it's Lavender? He could do better than some untried kid. Who's ever heard of Mark Bannister? Harry could afford the best writer in the country to tell his life and crimes to. Maybe someone else was feeding the kid the information. Any number of people could be doing it, for any number of reasons.'

'You, for example,' I said evenly.

'Pardon?'

'You. You seem to know so much about him. Maybe it was you feeding Mark the information.'

'Now look, you may be just testing the water but let's get one thing clear right here and now.' He jabbed his finger at me. 'If and when I write a book about Harry Lavender it'll have my name on it. I won't be hiding behind some two-bit kid with an artificial heart. And I know so much about Lavender because it's my business to know, OK?'

He wasn't angry, he wasn't emotional. He was telling me how things were. I was sorry now I'd said it, sorry I'd forgotten there were still people like Collier in the world.

'Same again?' I said, pointing to his glass.

'No thanks,' he said, standing up, 'I've got to get back to work.' He buttoned up his jacket. 'If I were you I'd take a good long holiday. Preferably out of the country. And I'd take it before someone put me permanently on holidays.'

I sat in the car and didn't switch on the ignition. I looked up and down the street in the rear vision mirror. It was a one-way street and the only way out was past a little row of decaying terraces. No one was walking along the street except for a couple who turned into the pub. Somewhere a dog barked. Behind that was the humming of the city. Harry Lavender's city.

I had eyes and ears in every pore of my skin. Something about the rubber on the side window was wrong. It was rippled, as if someone had been trying to lever it off. Or had succeeded.

I checked the glove box. Nothing moved. The pedals checked out and the dash looked innocuous. I got out and checked the fenders and the rest of the car. No transmitters. Then I lifted the hood and looked at the engine. Nobody hit me over the head with a blunt object and I couldn't find anything that looked like a bomb.

I got back in the car. Sooner or later I was going to have to turn on the ignition. I thought about my life. I'd had the husband, the kids, the career. What I would have liked was another 50 years.

I had to do it. I had to put the key in the ignition and turn.

I concentrated *ki,* breath energy, in my abdomen and exhaled forcefully. Did it for a full ten minutes till the shouting and the tumult died.

Then I turned the key.

The car started purring. I wiped my clammy hands on my knees and put on the indicator. No one else put on theirs. I slid out onto the road and before getting to the crest of the hill tried the brakes. They were perfect.

By the time I got to the crest I'd decided it was kids. Not that they were stupid enough to try a car as conspicuous as a '58 Daimler but sometimes bits went missing.

Though what kid would want to souvenir a piece of window rubber?

Halfway down the hill I put the brakes on again.

A car came up behind me. Full pelt.

An inch away from my back bumper bar it swerved and shot into a side street.

A black Porsche.

I proceeded down the hill and looked up the side street. The car had disappeared.

The sins of the father . . . Guy's baby . . . *he threatened to cut Guy's wife and baby. . . the knife slicing open the fly screen* . . . the sins of the mother . . . my babies . . .

I didn't go straight home, I went to a public phone box.

I listened to the beeps and a voice hundreds of miles away.

'Gary? It's Claudia.' . . . 'Yeah, fine.' . . . 'Nothing much. Just the usual.'

The usual beating up of security guards, the usual eyes watching and waiting, the usual sweat popping out of porous skin, the usual intrusions into my room. The usual.

'Look, Gary, I've had a hard day, all right?' I bit my lip, but the words and the shrill tone of them had already gone along the cables.

'Are the kids there? I'd like to talk to them.'

To hear their voices, to know my flesh and blood was safe. My babies.

'But it's late. Shouldn't they be home from school by now?' The usual tightness in the stomach, the usual adrenalin scouring the body.

'No, Gary, I'm fine. Just a hard day. You know what the city's like.'

Keep them home. Don't let them go to school, don't let them go riding, keep them safe, Gary, keep them from Har . . . from harm.

'Oh of course, the school bus.' Time and roads are slow in the country.

'No, Gary, really. I just wanted to say hello.' ... 'Yeah. In the school holidays. I'll be at the airport.' ... 'I bet they are, they even get to go in the cockpit.'

Don't send them down. Keep them out of this place. He owns it, owns everyone. How can you be sure ... the hostess ... keep them, Gary, hold them to your heart and never let them go.

I was standing on the edge of the blue light teetering, shot up, overdosed, the ganglia overloaded and the circuits shorting. I had to perform lobotomy, to incise the brain, slice it open and expurgate.

Who else would know he was dying of cancer? If a journalist knew, who else?

Those bold black letters were made by a computer printer. On which of the thousands of computers in the city had they been written? Mark's? Harry Lavender's? What about Ronny O'Toole? Even a child could use a computer. A child like Sally.

He was leaving me alone but he was not leaving me alone. He was not beating up my body, he was beating up my nerves, one malignant finger after the other weighted on the pressure points, screeching discordance playing on the nerve strings.

A system of unarmed combat using hands and feet. But not just hands and feet. The harmony of mind, body and spirit, the concentration of these to a point of bright light, intense and cutting as a laser. Hours in America – I could do it then – sitting in the pose of the warrior, pulling *ki* down into the body. The breath, the energy of the universe of which every living thing is merely a pulse, a beat of the central heart. Legs burning with pain and focussing on that pain, transforming it to red energy, to power, building spiritual armour, emptying the mind of everything else except that bright pearl of light, the target, the bull's-eye you could hit blindfolded, the arrow that could go through walls and find its mark.

I breathed open the channels, breathed in the ascending light and breathed out the brooding darkness. I punched at the shadows, punched them out and away, and away again, till the force field was shimmering.

Then I entered the program.

The room was full of afternoon light. Time had passed, the sun had shifted, or rather the earth had shifted in relation to the sun. In the thin eye membrane where the inner and outer connect, I could feel it.

I had to get into the system. I knew it could be done and I knew who could do it.

I placed the receiver back on the phone, picked it up again and called Otto.

'It's Claudia.' ... 'Yes, fine. Haven't got time for that now, I've got a job for you, a big one. You'll be paid. Out of my expenses. Remember when we went to that flat in Bondi the other night? Yes, with the modem. I want you to break into a system.' ... 'I *know* you're not a hacker but you know how to do it.' ... 'Don't talk to me about ethics. It's open slather out there. The system I want you to break into has no ethics.' ... 'Program your computer to run through random phone numbers.' ... 'OK, data transmission numbers. When we get to the next stage I'll have more information for you.' ... 'Don't fob me off with that. It's not *your* time, it's the computer's.' ...'You don't have that many customers. OK, clients. Stop being so wishy-washy, you know you'll love it.'

I knew Otto like a brother. It was just a hypocritical front. Like all the boys, he just LOVED drama.

There was a tougher system to get into, one that Otto with all his expertise couldn't help me with, a system that called for completely different tactics. The nervous system of Sally Villos.

'Sally? It's Claudia. Claudia Valentine.' She didn't hang up.

'How are you?' She was much better thank you, and apologised for her abruptness the other day. Would I like to come over for a drink?

It was too easy, too easy by far.

In the city I rented another car. After the little incident with the transmitter I was changing cars more often than I changed my underwear.

I could have picked a better time than six to be wending my way across the Harbour Bridge. The peak hour traffic was thick and only eased up after Manly. I was grateful I didn't have to join the lemmings every day.

The Sally that answered the door this time was a very cool little number. The make-up had a signature, as did the earrings, lace blouse and black tube skirt. It was cocktail time. Happy hour.

The heavily glossed lips parted. 'I thought you weren't coming.'

'Got caught up in the traffic.'

'Come in.'

I came in, past the mirrors, to the living room, and remembered to sit on the edge of the lounge chair.

'Scotch?'

'Just mineral water thanks.'

'Oh,' she said, disappointed, but she poured me one anyway. And a tequila for herself.

'Have you heard from your parents?'

'I got a postcard from them this morning. From Italy. I'm so envious. Italy must be so romantic.'

'I'm sure it is.' I sipped at the mineral water.

'How are your investigations going?'

'We're getting there.'

'Sounds awfully glamorous.'

No. It didn't. It sounded bland and non-committal. The conversation was beginning to sound like two actors reading scripts from different plays. It was my turn now to read from mine.

'What sort of car do you drive, Sally?'

'Daddy left me the Porsche,' she said, crunching on a bit of ice. 'It's in the garage at the moment, something wrong with the brakes. I nearly ran up the back of this big old car today. Nearly killed myself.'

And nearly killed me, I thought. A coincidence. A coinciding. She was playing me and I didn't like it. That wasn't all I didn't like. I didn't like *her*.

Cute, flighty and ultimately dangerous.

'Mark's sister told me you moved his things over here.'

'Yes, yes,' she said brightly. 'They're in my bedroom. Would you like to have a look?'

The bedroom was large, with pale pink walls and a single bed, her childhood bed, with a large teddy bear leaning back on the pillows. Beside the bed was a photo of a bride and groom.

'These your parents?'

'Yes,' she said.

I studied the photo. The man and woman were only a few years older than Sally was now. She didn't look like either of them, though beneath the mask of make-up she could have been anybody's daughter.

She handed me a packet tied in red tape. 'These are his papers. The clothes are in the wardrobe.'

There was a driver's licence, birth certificate and passport. I opened the passport and Mark's face stared out at me. I could still see the kid that mucked around at the bus stop. A healthy, youthful face, despite the heroin, more alive in the photograph than it should have been because now he was dead. Sally saw it too and looked away.

Apart from the multiple entry visa for the United States, the passport was clean.

'Was Mark planning to travel?'

'Yes, we were going to go to the States. To New York.'

'Are you still going to go?'

'I could,' she said, playing with a loose thread in the bedspread, 'but it wouldn't be the same now. Maybe in a while, when all this ... when my parents get back.' She stretched into a pose on the bed, still playing with the bedspread, the pearly nails making whorls. 'New York's the place, I could really make a name for myself there.'

Out of the corner of my eye I watched her catch glimpses of herself in the mirror, turning her face to the better profile. I had a strong desire to pick her up and shake the shit out of her.

The next item was an address book. It had very few entries and they were mainly first names.

Under H was a number with no name.

'Whose number is this?'

She stuck out her well-glossed bottom lip and shrugged her shoulders. 'Doesn't ring a bell.'

I looked at her sharply: the pun was unintentional.

'Didn't you ever get curious about it?'

'Mark's address book was no concern of mine,' she said, running her thumb along her fingernails in an offhand, world-weary manner.

I continued leafing through, wondering why she was letting me do this. On the inside back cover were two marks where sticky tape had been, as if an extra page had been stuck in. I looked for traces of words on the inside back cover but it was smooth as a baby's bum. I asked her but with a pout and another shrug she said she knew nothing about it.

I closed the address book and handed it back to her. 'Let's have a look at the clothes.'

She opened an extremely messy wardrobe that was quite at odds with the rest of the house. Obviously the cleaning lady's limits had been defined for her. There was one dinner suit, some Adidas running shoes, jeans and brightly coloured shirts. I started going through the pockets.

'I . . . I've already done that,' said Sally sheepishly.

It was all right to go through pockets but not address books. 'Find anything?'

'Only some loose change.' She gazed wistfully at the clothes. I shut the door on them.

The sound system was neat and compact. Laser disc stuff. I opened everything that would open and wasn't screwed down.

'Looks like pretty expensive stuff. Where did he get it from?'

'Oh,' she said vaguely, 'someone got it for him duty free.'

'Who?' I was having a hard time keeping her away from the mirror.

She swallowed. 'Just someone. I don't know.'

The computer sat on her desk smiling its blank innocent smile.

'Do you know how to operate one of those things?'

'No, I'm not very good with technology.'

I bit my tongue in time to stop a smart comment to the precious child. Then I noticed that the computer was plugged in. Why was it plugged in if she didn't know how to operate it?

'Didn't you do Computer Studies at school?'

'No, I did Art.'

Oh God.

'There seems to be something missing, Sally – the fit.'

She swung her legs over into a sitting position. 'I threw it away. It wasn't exactly the sort of thing you want to keep.'

I was sick of playing her game. Now I played mine.

'Did you do heroin too?'

She looked at me, perishing the thought.

'Did you ever shoot him up? It would be easy for a doctor's daughter to get syringes.'

Beneath the mask the eyes were flickering. 'I didn't have anything to do with that!'

'But you didn't mind advertising the fact that Mark did. You brought it up at the funeral and you brought it up again when I came here.'

'So? There's nothing special about it. A lot of people do smack.'

'But they don't all die,' I spat back at her.

She looked at me knowingly, the hint of a smile on the edges of the lipstick, a look that said I know something you don't. 'Mark was one of the ones who did.'

'You don't seem particularly perturbed.'

'Well, what do you expect? Mark's dead but I'm not. I have to keep living.'

Yes, we all have to keep living. For as long as we can. Even when you're wading through mud and it all stinks, you have to keep going.

She flounced off the bed and came back with the tequila, and like a defiant child took a slug straight from the bottle. She looked at me like she wanted to kill me.

But it would take more than her eyes to kill me. And her Porsche.

I tried to soften those eyes. 'Why do you think he did all that stuff?' I asked quietly.

'He was . . . he was like that. Hyper . . . kind of paranoid. He said it calmed him down, nothing was ever a problem when he had the smack. He used to worry a lot. About the manuscript. Thought someone might steal it. Steal all his work.'

It was the most believable thing she'd said so far. I'd been so concerned about my university thesis being lost or stolen I'd never let it out of the house. When I did eventually finish it and had to take it out to be photocopied I caught a cab. If I'd had the money to hire an Armaguard van I would have. I sat in the back clutching the thesis to my breast waiting for the accident to happen. It didn't matter if I died as long as the manuscript was safe. When I got to the photocopier's I wouldn't leave it, I had to do it myself. All 120 pages of it, four copies. I smiled to myself. Who would want to steal 120 pages of waffle on 'Syntactic Structures of Australian Idiom'?

But someone might want to steal Mark's.

'So there was a manuscript.'

She nodded. 'Not on paper, on a computer disc.'

I looked about the room. 'So where is it now?'

'I thought you might know that.'

'Why would I know?'

'Because . . . because . . . aren't you taking charge of his affairs or something? I thought you might have found out where it is.'

'Well, I haven't.'

She looked oddly relieved.

'Where are his discs?'

'There weren't any.'

'What do you mean, there weren't any? He needed discs for the computer, didn't he?'

'Of course. I don't know what happened to them. When I moved his stuff over there were no discs.'

'But he must have had a print-out, a copy somewhere.'

She shrugged her shoulders. 'I don't know. Why should he?'

'Writers usually do, you know.' Apart from the paranoia it was a reasonable thing to do. Who'd spend months working on something without some sort of back-up? Is that why Mark was paranoid? Because he had nearly finished his book and the only record he had of it was a piece of plastic? But there was the modem. Copies could be stored elsewhere. I wondered how Otto was getting on.

'What do you know about the book?'

'What's there to know? To tell you the truth, I wasn't all that interested.' She sounded nonchalant but her hands were still picking bits out of the bedspread. And she still couldn't drag herself away from the mirror.

'But it was going to be a best-seller. Didn't that arouse your interest?'

She sighed and looked straight at me. 'They were all going to be best-sellers. I don't suppose he'd have kept on writing if he didn't believe that.'

'Did you believe it?'

She turned her eyes away and looked at the mounting pile of threads. I wondered how she was going to explain a bald bedspread to her parents.

'No, not really. He'd get all enthusiastic about something, and then when I'd ask him how it was going he'd say, "Oh that, that's history", as if I was a moron or something for even asking. "I've got another idea for a book and this is going to be it!" That's what he said every time, or words to that effect.' She breathed out heavily. 'I loved Mark but can you blame me for not having faith in his work? He just never finished anything. Great ideas, no staying power.'

'But,' I gently reminded her, 'he had finished this one, hadn't he, or was close to it.'

'Yes, but this one was different,' she blurted out. Oh, if only she could stop the tape and delete.

'How was this one different?'

'Just different, that's all.'

'"Just different" is not good enough, Sally.'

'Why are you asking me all this stuff, anyway? Aren't you just supposed to . . . to assess the value of his things or something?'

It was a bit late in the conversation for her to be asking this now.

'Mark was murdered, Sally, did you know that?'

'*Murdered?*' She said it as if it was a word from a foreign language. 'Mark wasn't murdered, it was an accident. He wasn't murdered, he wasn't!' She hammered the message into the bear. 'He couldn't have been. It was the smack. He couldn't have been murdered, murder is what . . . is what criminals do . . .'

'And innocent people are often the victims,' I reminded her.

I held her hands and made her look at me. She tried to pull away. She was surprisingly strong, but I held.

'OK, OK, maybe he was murdered and maybe it was an accident. If he was murdered – let's just say he was murdered – wouldn't you want the murderer brought to justice?' The words nearly curled in my mouth.

She thought about it. For a fraction too long for the outburst to be spontaneous.

'No. No!' Then softer, as if she'd seen my eyes, 'Would that make any difference? Why don't you leave it alone? I just want it to stop!'

This was the second time today I'd been advised to leave it alone. It made me more determined not to leave it alone. Besides, I was too involved now to let go. The arrow was already in the air, moving inexorably towards the target. Too late now to reel it back in. Even if I wanted to. But I didn't want to. I would get Lavender. If it was the last thing I did. Get him for what he'd done to my father. For what he was doing to my city.

She'd nearly finished the bottle now and the mask was coming undone. Mascara ran down her cheeks and the blood-red lipstick was smudged from nose to chin. She looked like a clown.

'Sally,' I said softly. 'Sally.' I bent down level with her. She pulled her head away. 'I'd like to take the computer away with me. Would that be all right?'

'No. No, it wouldn't,' she said, trying to cut me with her eyes. 'It's Mark's. You can't have it.'

'It would only be for a day or so.' Only long enough for Otto to go to work on it.

'No,' she said sullenly.

'I can get a court order for it.'

'Get it, then,' she sneered.

I breathed and counted to ten. Several times.

'Well, what are you waiting for? You know the way out.'

Yes, I knew the way out.

I tossed her a tube of Beroccas. 'Here, have these. They're great for the hangover you're going to have.'

I slammed the security door shut and walked down the steps to the car. Except for the sound of the surf a few blocks away the street was quiet. I wondered how many other women were sitting behind security doors drinking tequila and watching re-runs of *Days of Our Lives*.

I wondered too whether there were any undigested grains of truth in this load of horse shit she'd just piled on me.

Driving back over the Bridge I thought about the mess I'd just left, and thought about my job. You did get to look behind the facades, behind the security doors, and it wasn't always pretty.

There were a lot worse things to do in life: I could be a doctor telling a cancer patient he had six months to live, even if that patient were cancer himself like Harry Lavender. Or I could be a social worker taking to court a parent who beats up on a child. I provided a service. People could take it or leave it, I didn't ram it down their necks.

By the time I got to North Sydney I'd almost convinced myself.

I slid off the Bridge into the city, heading west. Passing under the Monorail felt like walking under a ladder but there was no way to avoid it. The metal snake was now part of the city. I zoomed across Darling Harbour and took in the ever-shifting sights. And sites. Gleaming new metal and the maze of scaffolding, the signs of those who had won the tenders, bright clean signs belying the wheeling and dealing that had put them there, the palm trees lining the new avenues, transplanted fully grown from the places where they'd been planted, like old bull elephants uprooted from jungles to be caged in zoos for people to gawp at. I tried to picture what all this had looked like a few short years ago but couldn't. Like everyone else, I would accept it once it was a *fait accompli,* vaguely aware that the signposts of the city's history and my own were being effaced, as if someone had gone through my photo album and replaced the photos of me with those of another child, more modern, better dressed.

Traffic was banked up on the approach to Glebe Island Bridge. A container vessel was leaving port, the same vessel that had witnessed my altercation with the security guard. From halfway round the world water had carried it right up the veins into the heart of this city. Blue water that here was green at the edges and hid a multitude of sins. Water absorbs everything: schemes gone awry, dumped cargo, bodies, gold wedding rings, a child's first thong, they all lay on the bottom beneath the placid levelling surface. Just like the reminders of the city's past levelled by the developers of the future.

Everything stank of Lavender.

The city was highly strung, a girl like Sally, a beautiful, made-up face, a sophisticated child, cool and crying and laughing all in the one breath, a liar, a tease. A girl craning her neck to see her reflection in the mirror or glass buildings. The nerves run riot by the jagging edge of jackhammers.

More than four million people crowded into this city while the rest of the continent remained a vacant lot. Because here the isolation was less intense, here you could stand on the foreshores and gaze out to sea and know that just beyond the horizon lay another country. Even if it was only New Zealand.

'**G**ive us a Scotch, Jack.'

The after-work crowd was in full swing. There was that dull rumble of male voices, punctuated by the muted click of balls hitting together in the pool room. And not just the balls on the table. Men in jeans and T-shirts lined up shots, resting their cigarettes and beer on the cushion, muttered under their breaths when they missed the easy ones and tried to look nonchalant when they pulled off a tricky one. Smoke filled the room and the laughter was wicked. It was what my grandmother would call a 'den of iniquity'.

Out here it was more like a din of inequity. I squeezed onto a bar stool besides two solicitors arguing over something in the *Financial Review*. Up the end of the bar sat George in his flares and nylon windcheater, muttering to himself and reading the evening paper with a rather shaky finger. Every pub had a George. He was there morning, noon and night and never seemed to eat, apart from salt-and-vinegar chips. 'Never missed a day,' he would tell you if you were unlucky enough to get into conversation with him. 'I've been coming here for thirty-five years and never missed a day.' He had a wife at home but no one ever saw her. Rumour had it that he and his wife never spoke to each other. When their only son was killed in action in Korea they still didn't speak. She just left the telegram on the kitchen table for him to see. Both hugging their individual grief, too locked up in their isolated cells to share it.

He caught my eye and gave me a silent salute. His mouth moved into something resembling a smile but the blackened teeth detracted somewhat from its charm. I returned him a disinterested closed-mouth one, the sort that issues no invitation but still George lumbered towards me, armed with the newspaper.

'Now, George, don't annoy the customers.'

'I'm not a customer,' I said. 'I live here.'

'And so does he. Unfortunately,' said Jack under his breath.

George didn't really bother me. I was curious about him, curious to know whether Guy had gone like this before he'd finally taken to the streets. He was always pointing out ghoulish bits in the paper, almost gleefully, as if life really was the shit sandwich on three-day-old white bread he thought it was. People didn't really listen to George, merely nodded their heads politely, hoping he'd go away. '. . . and just a young bloke too . . . good swimmer . . . had his legs broken . . .'

'Yes, George, terrible, isn't it?' I smiled politely.

Then it started to sink in.

'Can I see that, George?'

He had his finger under bold black letters:

SURFER DEAD ON BONDI BEACH

I raced through it, through the body and the broken legs looking for the name.

It jumped out at me and pulled me down like a drowning man.

The name was Robbie Macmillan.

'Excuse me.'

I walked towards the toilets with measured steps, smiling politely at the clusters of suits I had to squeeze past. One more second, Claudia, just one more.

Then I locked myself in, reeling like a maniac, leaning against the door to stop myself falling down. I saw the broken swimmer swimming uselessly for the shore, the rough waves pushing him back and back, the mouth finally opening to take in the wide brown sea . . .

I knew why people retched and gagged. Because there were some things you couldn't stomach. Why the eyes streamed. Because you couldn't hold it in. Why they raved and ranted and went mad. Because the message to the computer in the skull was just too much and the system revolted.

Why was Robbie's body lying broken on the beach, the bloody irony of the beach that was home to him? An innocent bystander the crims reckon they don't kill. But they'd killed Robbie, they'd killed Robbie.

And I knew just who had put the boot in.

I flushed the toilet and put the seat down. The blaze subsided, turning into a cold hard lump where the heart used to be.

'**C**arol? It's Claudia.' . . . 'I'm alive and kicking.' And so was someone else.

'That body that was found at Bondi. It was Johnny the Jumper.' . . . 'Don't be pedantic, I just know.'

They knew too but didn't have 'proof'.

'Bring him in, Carol. The bastard's a maniac.' . . . 'I don't know what charge. Use your imagination. Maybe he's got bald tyres. Just get him, Carol. Get him.'

I had another call to make – the nameless number in Mark Bannister's address book. It rang twice, then the trill turned into something else, something I'd never heard before. It was not engaged and it was not disconnected. *Ming ming ming ming ming.* Burning my brain out from the inside like a microwave.

'Otto? The data transmission number – I've got it.' I could almost feel Lavender breathing down my neck.

As soon as I slammed the receiver down the phone started ringing. I wrenched it up again. There was heavy breathing. I'd had this kind of call before.

'Put it away, you wanker!' I shouted and slammed it down again.

It rang again almost immediately.

This time the heavy breathing had turned into sobbing. I'd heard that before, too.

'Sally? Did you just ring me? What's wrong?' . . . 'Don't move, I'll be over right away. Don't answer the phone and don't answer the door till I get there.'

I had a sort of inverted Midas touch. Everyone who talked to me about Mark was turning into a corpse or a screaming heap. Two down, how many more to go?

Who else had I contaminated? Who else was fallible? *Perhaps in the connection to the heart . . . the slender thread between the fallible and the infallible . . .*

Oh dear God, no, not Steve. Not Steve, the connection to the heart, the slender thread. I had to hear his voice, to know he was OK, that he hadn't been touched.

I sat staring at the phone. I couldn't move. It was ringing with laughter, that horrible echoing laughter like the demon in a horror movie.

What if Steve hadn't been touched? If he was alive and well and unkicked?

I nearly killed him . . . one particular program and his heart went haywire . . . phone tapping . . . so sophisticated now there's no way of telling . . .

He knew how to do it.

Maybe . . . Lucifer was once an angel . . . no, oh no, not Steve . . .

I willed myself to pick up the phone. If I heard his voice I would know.

I dialled each digit hard and deliberately. A wrong number would be a bad omen.

I didn't hear his voice. I heard the phone ringing and ringing and ringing.

By the looks of Sally she'd poured half the duty free shop down her throat. The tequila and Scotch bottles were empty and so was a bottle of cooking sherry. I went into the kitchen and made her a cup of coffee.

'Ugh!' she said. 'No milk.'

'It's better that way. Now, what happened?'

'It's you, it's your fault,' she screamed at me. 'It happened because of you!'

She pushed me away violently. 'Don't touch me! Get out of here, I never want to see you again!'

'Sally,' I said softly enough to get under the pitch of her voice, 'you called me, remember? I'm here because you called.'

'Who else could I call?' she screamed.

If I still smoked, now would have been the time to light one up.

'OK, try telling me about it.'

I waited. Waited all the time it took for her to calm down enough to be coherent.

It didn't take as long as I expected.

'Not long after you left two men came. When I opened the door they pushed me back into the house. One of them told me to sit down and the other one started looking in all the rooms. When he came to my room he called out to the other one. The other one made me stand up and walk in front of him. He had a gun and he stuck it in my back. He stuck a gun in my back . . .'

A pity he hadn't pulled the trigger.

'What happened when you got to your room?' The words came out like cold hard stones.

She blew her nose.

'It was dreadful. All Mark's things were all over the place . . .'

'Let's go and have a look.'

Everything *was* all over the place. Everything except the computer.

'Did they take it?'

She nodded.

'They . . . they said something strange. They said, "We're repo men, the owner didn't keep up with his payments." Then they laughed, like it was a joke or something.'

'Did they take anything else?'

'No . . . just the computer.'

Of course the computer, of course. Conveniently before Claudia could have it examined more closely, of course.

'What did they look like?'

'Like businessmen. One was young and the other old, about 40.'

'Was the older one wearing driving gloves?'

She paused, consulting the script. 'They both wore gloves.'

'Did you see what sort of car they were driving?'

'I'm not sure. Before I answered the door I looked out the window. There was a white car, some sort of Japanese one, I don't know which, parked across the road but I don't know if it was theirs.'

'Didn't they get into it when they left?'

'I . . . I don't know. I was too upset to think about looking. I just phoned you.'

'When will your parents be back?'

'In a couple of weeks.'

'Couldn't you go and stay with friends till then?'

'I guess so,' she said without much conviction.

'I don't expect those men will be back if they've got what they want, but it's better to be on the safe side. Ring and let me know where you'll be.'

I didn't expect those men back. I didn't expect they'd been there in the first place.

'And Sally, go easy on the bottle. It makes you start imagining all sorts of things.'

headed for the city. Again. Underneath the make-up and the act Sally *was* erratic, highly strung. Just who was tautening those strings of hers? Sooner or later she'd slip up – if she hadn't already. OK, there was an outside chance that she'd had visitors after I'd left. And that they'd taken the computer. And dropped it off somewhere.

It was 11 pm and the movies were just coming out. A group of pasty-faced boys entered the games arcade. The doorman stepped aside for them. It wasn't the Maori.

But I wasn't interested in the games or the Maori, just the arcade. Especially the exterior.

The facade was new but the building was old. There were security signs on the window. If I tried to enter by the ground floor doors or windows I'd be walking through a minefield.

But nobody ever thought of securing the roof. No-one ever thought of roofs at all. In this city all anyone thought of was facades.

The arcade had probably been a warehouse at some stage. It had an upper storey whose only illumination was the street light. The interior looked as dead as a doornail. But appearances can be deceiving – many an illegal casino was housed in boarded-up top floors. Even in gentrified Balmain, to say nothing of the city.

On top of this was a tiled roof. Hopefully some of those tiles would be in need of repair. Cracked, broken, easy to prise off.

All the buildings adjoined one another. You could probably go the whole block roof-hopping. And never be seen, not even in daylight. People in the city never look up.

The night was perfect, not a cloud in the sky. No stars either but the city makes it own. It was the sort of night when people would stay out late, damn it. It could have been worse. It could have been raining with all the surfaces wet and slippery. Nasty things, slippery tiles.

Though the big cinema complexes were closing there was a small one across the road that showed late night cult movies for the diehards. The session finished at 3.10 am. I paid my money and went in.

I'd seen the movie six times already. The seventh time I was looking but not really listening. I was thinking about Harry Lavender and Mark Bannister, about Ronny O'Toole and Robbie Macmillan, about Sally Villos and . . . ? About Steve Angell and . . . ? About Claudia Valentine and all of them.

I went into the 'Ladies'. My entry startled a young woman rolling a joint.

'Someone just laid some really great Queensland heads on me . . . they're *amazing* . . . far out . . .'

She was trying to manoeuvre what looked like a piece of cow cud onto the four papers she'd stuck together.

'Why don't you try rolling it in one of the cubicles? Then you won't be disturbed.' And neither would I.

'Oh, *right* . . .' she sang, stumbling into a cubicle.

'Hey, what about this?' I said, indicating the dope still sitting on the handbasin.

'Oh yeah,' she said, hitting her forehead with the flat of her hand, 'I'm really out of it.'

Her eyes were swimming and she couldn't wipe the grin off her face. At this rate it would take her all night. If she didn't pass out first.

I did front kicks, side kicks, back kicks. Punches to the head, the solar plexus and the groin.

I was just about to chop the soap in half when I heard: 'Hey, that's amazing. Can you really do that?'

I walked out of the 'Ladies' and into the darkness, thinking about the strange things you see in midnight cinemas.

Things were considerably quieter in the streets this time round. Soon the street cleaners would be along, swishing the streets with water. The sound of the dead of night.

The arcade was closed now with just a night light, the cinemas and shops the same. Dimly lit interiors behind closed doors. Hardly inviting. But sometimes you had to invite yourself.

I drove the hire car into the dark alley just right for a mugging, behind the games arcade. Several of the buildings, including the arcade, had big double doors on the upper storey. On the arcade doors hung a heavy chain with a hook. Standing on the roof of the car I could probably swing myself up there. The timber of the doors looked weathered. With luck I wouldn't have to go on the roof at all. With luck.

I stuck my hair up into a beanie and pulled on a pair of silent joggers with good traction. And a pair of gloves. Then I took the tool-bag from the boot and slung it over my shoulder.

There were lights either end of the alley but no people. No people at all.

I climbed onto the roof of the car and reached for the hook, grabbed hold of it and scaled the crumbly brick wall, going all the way up to the ledge.

The doors were padlocked but looked like they would splinter at the first impact. Still holding onto the chain, I kicked. But they were more solid than they looked. My eyes scaled the wall right up to the roof. It was a long way up with few footholds. I took out the crowbar and kicked again. There was a soft tearing sound. But not enough. Mind, body and soul, the concentration of these to a point of bright light. Intense and cutting as a laser. I breathed deeply and on the exhalation tried again. This time a section splintered off the bottom. Enough to crawl through. I would like to have gone in head first but up here on the ledge I didn't have a lot of choice. I had to move quickly, to get in and out of sight. What I was doing halfway up a building with a crowbar would take some explaining should anyone start asking questions. Assuming that they would ask questions before pulling the trigger.

With my weight on the hook chain, I slid my legs in through the opening.

'Show me the way to go home, I'm tired and I wanna go to bed. Well, I had a little drink . . .'

I froze. Remained motionless, hoping the pounding of my heart wasn't making the whole street vibrate. I wasn't so worried about the drunk as about a passing patrol car that might come to investigate the noise.

Then the singing stopped. He was directly below me, patting

the car. He collapsed against it and lo and behold, the only person in Sydney to do it, he looked up.

I didn't blink.

'Hey!' he said, waving the bottle dangerously above him. 'Hey! Wife won't let you in? Same here mate, same here.'

I did not turn a hair. I sat staring at what was once the grain in the timber, waiting for the cops to come and slam him in the cooler for the night and me for much longer. Seconds lasted an eternity. I could hear the blood pumping through my veins, feel my hands sweating in the gloves, the cold metal of the chain, the night air on my back.

He was still there and what's worse, he'd started singing again.

I turned my head as far as it would go.

'Psst!' To no avail.

'Psst!' It was so loud and long this time it sounded like a pressure cooker blowing its top.

The singing stopped and he looked up as if the clouds had parted and he'd just seen God.

I put my finger to my lips in a sh! gesture and pointed to the doors, like a drunk myself trying to avoid the clichéd wife with the clichéd rolling pin behind the clichéd door.

He grinned broadly in recognition and put his own finger to his lips, patted the car one last time, then moved on.

A sigh of relief. A last look down the lane. Then I was in.

The place looked like a morgue for dead games machines. They sat in rows like an assembled army of tanks, the metal edges gleaming ominously in the street light. In one corner was a pile of cartons. Empty.

I started with the machines in the darkest part of the room. I unscrewed the back panel of one and shone the torch. Onto microchips and a network of coloured wires. I wished I knew more about what I was looking at, wished I knew more about computers. I could see the way the world was turning and it was turning into a gigantic computer network. If you weren't electronically literate you might as well go and live in a hollow log.

The first few machines revealed nothing. I didn't have all night. I flashed the torch around machines that didn't look so dead.

Eventually I found something. No little packets of pure white and deadly but marks where adhesive tape had been.

Also, no computers.

It was time to try the 'office'.

The top step creaked when I stepped onto it. I drew back so far into the wall I was part of it, then pressed in doubly hard because downstairs was the dull thud of a door closing. I heard the sound of games machines being dragged along the floor. And voices.

'Don't bother unpacking. We've got business in the office.'

The other voice was indistinct, but there was the intonation of a question.

There was a chuckle.

A chuckle I'd heard before.

'Seems you've been drawing attention to yourself, taking things into your own hands. Now Harry doesn't like that. He likes things to be nice and quiet. Especially you.'

The other voice now came out in spurts of fear.

'Into the office, whitey, and none of your tricks. I can see in the dark.'

There was no mistaking that sliding voice. It was the Maori.

A thin shaft of light appeared from under the 'office' door but everything was as quiet as a nun. I couldn't risk any more creaking steps and stood there, unable to move.

After an eternity the door opened and the Maori came out. I waited for the other guy to come out. Waited and waited.

Silently, swiftly I made the descent.

Downstairs had the chill of a cemetery at midnight. If someone was still in that office they were either awfully quiet or awfully dead.

I slid along the wall and with one swift long kick opened the door fully.

The body was lying face down but I recognised the leather jacket, even with its intricate pattern of bullet holes.

It was O'Toole. Johnny the Jumper.

He was holding something in his hand, something pink and fleshy. I stared at it for quite a while before I could make out what it was.

And then I wished I hadn't.

I had to turn away before I vomited. O'Toole was holding his tongue.

When I opened my eyes again I saw a gun. It was lying on the floor a metre away from the body. I picked it up, carefully avoiding looking at the body and that thing in its hand. It wasn't this gun that had fired those bullets. It was still fully loaded, no spent cartridges. I put it down again in exactly the same position.

In front of the body was a huge desk. With a piece of wire from my tool-bag, I coaxed the drawers open. And struck a goldmine. There were shipping timetables, computer manuals, lists of figures. There were company titles – Lavender Blue Enterprises and Terminal Investments sprang out like attacking panthers. There was more. Property titles. And more. A finger in every pie. Hartronics, pacemaker manufacturers. Sydney Girl, modelling agency.

And there was more. There was a glossy magazine, face down. I turned it over and drew my breath. Staring back at me in black and white with red glossed lips was Sally.

A picture of Sally among Harry Lavender's titles. An odd juxtaposition. A coincidence. No, not odd. Not a coincidence. Perfectly in keeping, to find Sally among Harry Lavender's titles of ownership. I stared at the photo, willing it to life, willing it to tell me what it was doing there. In the silence of the frame in which the camera never lies the slightly parted lips seemed to murmur. Then shout, louder and louder:

I am Harry Lavender's daughter.

It was time to call the Law in. I dialled Carol's home number. Then the lights went out.

I was vaguely aware of a steady drone, the same sort of sound I heard every morning – the city revving up for the day. But I didn't feel like waking up. Images of police cars and ambulances floated in the shimmering light.

I was dead.

No. Not dead. You don't feel pain like this when you're dead. Don't feel your head's been split open like a ripe watermelon. In my mouth was the sour taste of alcohol. If this was a hangover it should go down in the *Guinness Book Of Records*.

I was cold and my feet were wet. My nose felt very negroid. It was rammed against the steering wheel of the hire car.

The shimmering light turned blue. Muddy blue. I hadn't seen it from quite this close before but the view looked familiar. I was off the edge of the park where I'd walked with Steve – out in the lapping waters of the harbour. The tide was out. Way way out.

I was putting one and one together and it wasn't coming out two.

Why did I smell like a brewery when I hadn't touched a drop of alcohol all night?

The last thing I remembered was dialling Carol's number.

YOU DON'T LOOK VERY WELL!

Why did he have to use a megaphone?

I wasn't well, at least I hoped I wasn't. I wouldn't want to be well and feel like this.

The ambulance people hoisted me back up to the park. I refused the stretcher. I wasn't going to take this lying down.

For some strange reason I assured them I was all right.

They drifted into the background and the blue uniforms came to the fore. They made me breathe into a bag. I must have passed with flying colours because they made me get into the car and 'accompany them to the police station'. There were two of them – one nice, one tough. They didn't look like they needed accompanying.

After the preliminary name, address and identification they made me blow into the bag again. This time the reading was way below the limit. The nice cop and the tough cop exchanged glances.

'Perhaps you'd like to give us your account of the events of last night,' said the nice one.

'Perhaps I would. But not to you. I'll speak to Detective Carol Rawlins.'

'Don't make things difficult for yourself, lady.'

It seemed to me they couldn't be very much more difficult than they already were.

'Call Detective Rawlins.'

The nice one narrowed his eyes and looked at me steadily. Underneath, even the nice ones are tough.

'You're only making things difficult for yourself.'

'Call Detective Rawlins!' I screamed.

The nice one dialled the number. The last thing they wanted was an hysterical female screaming police abuse.

All I had to do now was figure out what to say to Carol.

'Carol? Claudia here.' . . . 'Yes, well, I'd like to know what I'm doing here, too. I've got a statement but I want to give it to you. In person.'

There was silence on the other end of the line. I could tell Carol didn't like it but finally she agreed to see me.

'Great! Would you like to tell them?'

I handed the phone to the nice one. 'It's for you.'

He looked at me like I was a leper but eventually he took the phone.

'About ten minutes. Yes, leaving now.'

He hung up and ushered me out of the station.

'What about my car?'

'What about your car?'

'It doesn't swim very well. Maybe we should call a tow truck.'

'You'll need more than a tow truck, lady. C'mon.'

Carol's desk sergeant was drinking coffee. I needed one badly but not badly enough to drink that government muck.

'Detective Rawlins is expecting us.'

'Go right in,' said the desk sergeant.

Carol didn't look pleased to see me, especially flanked as I was by two of her colleagues, though I wasn't sure she'd call two suburban constables her 'colleagues'.

'Thank you,' she said.

My bodyguards didn't budge.

'You needn't stand on ceremony, boys, there are chairs outside.'

They backed out like they were leaving royalty. Or maybe they just didn't trust her. After all, she was a cop.

'OK . . .' she said wearily, though it was only eight o'clock in the morning.

'Those boys give you the rundown?'

'Yes. Drunk driving.'

'Did they also tell you about the discrepancy between the two readings?'

'Yes.' She frowned.

'I was set up.'

'Indeed. You hadn't been drinking at all?'

'I know you may find it hard to believe, but no.'

'Blackouts? That sort of thing?'

'No. Well, yes, there was one. Induced by a heavy object applied to the back of the head. I dialled your number and the next thing I knew I was paddling in the harbour.'

'What time was that?' Once a cop always a cop.

''Bout four in the morning. Now you know I wouldn't call you at that time of day without a good excuse.'

'Which was . . .?'

'A body. A very dead body.'

Her finely pencilled eyebrows shot up under her thick bang of hair.

'Anyone we know?'

'Ronny O'Toole. Otherwise known as Johnny the Jumper.'

Her face went through the gamut of emotions, the predominant one being dismay.

'Well, that saves the police a lot of trouble, doesn't it? But it may bring us more. He's one of Harry Lavender's thugs.'

'I know.'

'I hope you also know it doesn't look very good for you. You phone telling me, no, *ordering* me to get him and the next day he's dead. Now what's the dead boy got to do with the dead man?'

'The boy talked to someone. About heroin.'

'Well, that fits. Heroin was found in Macmillan's home.'

Now it was my turn to run the emotional gamut. My brain refused to accept this new bit of information. 'No,' I said, my heart down around my ankles, 'Robbie wasn't involved . . . it must have been a plant.'

A Lavender plant.

'All right, Claudia, start at the beginning and don't leave out the details. I want everything. *Everything.*'

My head was hurting like hell. Even thinking made it feel like any minute now it was going to break open like a soft boiled egg. With a similar gooey mess oozing out.

'Could I have a cup of coffee?' I was desperate but I needed the caffeine.

She sighed heavily but ordered the coffee. I gulped half of it down and tried not to screw up my face. It felt pretty screwed up anyway.

I started at the beginning and gave Carol details. Not all of them, but enough to give her good reasons for my presence at the scene of the crime.

'You realise breaking and entering is a criminal offence.'

'I think murder takes precedence. Just pretend you never heard me say how I got in there.'

'You know I can't do that.'

'You can. You didn't get to sit behind that big shiny desk by always doing it by the book.'

She spread well manicured fingers along that desk. 'Your long term memory, as always, is impeccable. But may I remind you, Ms Valentine, that I *am* sitting behind this big shiny desk and you are in front of it. So before I throw you to those lions out there, shall we get down to business?' She'd come a long way from Bankstown.

She leant back in her chair and asked for more precise times and layout. Then she sent two cops round to the arcade.

'You don't expect the body to still be there, do you?'

'Not really, specially as no one's reported it. But there should be signs.'

'Got a search warrant?'

She sighed. 'Yes, Claudia, we've got a search warrant.'

'If Lavender's involved you'll need it.'

'Lavender's been lying low lately.'

'Beautiful alliteration, Carol. Old Copperhead would be proud of you.'

She smiled, nearly chuckled, in spite of her well-tailored suit and big shiny desk. Then her work face came back on.

'Why would he have his own man killed?'

'Because of Macmillan. The Jumper's bringing Lavender more publicity than he wants right now.'

'So you've heard the rumour.'

'Yeah, I've heard the rumour.'

'Hmm. There's something that intrigues me,' she said, carefully placing her fingers together. 'You know how much exercise the Jumper needs to keep fit. How come, if he's been following you, you haven't had any aggravation?'

'I wouldn't exactly call last night a tea party! I was set up for that.'

'Before that. He was already dead when you had your "tea party". If you've been nosing around Lavender's business, how come you're still alive? Maybe he's sick but he's not dead.'

My brain was tugging at my skirts to go home, like a child unable to cope with the adults' conversation.

'That's what I'd like to know. Could be he's saving me up for something special.'

'It doesn't look good, Claudia, I'm telling you now.'

'Maybe that's what they're aiming for. To make me not look good. Hoping that given enough rope I'll not only hang myself but trip over it in the process. They're not stupid and they've had plenty of opportunities.

'Can I go now? I've got some rest to catch up on.'

'I think it's best if you stay. At least till my sergeants report back. You can lie down in the cell if you like.'

'No thanks.' I knew how comfortable the bunk in the cell would be, and I wasn't going to let myself be tricked into going behind bars. 'Not unless you want to arrest me.'

'Hopefully that won't be necessary.' I'd been joking but Carol wasn't. 'Can I get you anything?'

'A lobotomy would be great but I'd settle for a couple of Panadol.'

She opened a drawer and produced a packet. 'Glass of water?'

'I'll wash it down with the coffee.'

'I don't know how you can drink that stuff. I never touch it.'

'At least it's a change from water. I woke up in water this morning and I've had enough for one day.'

'Very amusing,' she said, decidedly unamused. 'Now if you don't mind, I've got work to do.'

Maybe I was imagining it but for some reason my presence here was annoying the shit out of Carol. I was too far below par to wonder why. I'd think about it later. Think about it all later.

We sat in heavy silence. I leafed through a glossy magazine for businesswomen and Carol got on with her work. Paper work.

The silence was interrupted by the quiet buzz of her telephone.

'Detective Rawlins speaking.' She had pen and paper at the ready.

'Hmm, how convenient.' . . . 'Didn't think so but we could get someone to check it out.' . . . 'Break in from upstairs, eh?' she said, shooting me with her eyes.

'Who did you speak to?' . . . 'And there was no one else there?'. . . 'Uh-huh. And the office?'. . . 'Uh-huh.' . . . 'OK, come and see me when you come back.'

She replaced the receiver and spread her hands out on the table. It was getting more like the headmistress' office every minute.

'They came, they saw, but they didn't conquer. There was evidence of a break-in but nothing else.'

'Nothing at all?'

'That's right. No body, no nothing. The office as neat as a pin. Doesn't look good, does it?'

'But I *saw* it! I was ringing you about it!'

'Was that before or after the Scotch?'

The remark pierced as sharp as the pain in my head.

'Carol, I told you what happened! Would I be calling you about murder if there wasn't any body?'

'You didn't call,' she said dryly.

'For God's sake, Carol, I was on the phone to you when I got hit on the head by an unidentified blunt object. Do you think this mess is self-inflicted? What about the blood-stained carpet?'

'There was no carpet.'

'Well, that proves it, doesn't it? Away getting the blood-stains removed.'

'Not necessarily. Don't you ever send your rugs away to be dry-cleaned?'

'I don't own rugs,' I said defiantly. 'Do you?'

'I have the odd one or two.'

'Of course! You must be doing all right on your detective's salary.'

'I am.'

The silence roared like thunder.

'C'mon Carol, it's obvious. They've removed the body and they've removed the evidence.'

'What may be obvious to one person is not necessarily obvious to another,' she said evenly.

'Carol! I can't believe this. Do you think all this is a bullshit story?'

She sighed. 'No, Claudia, quite frankly I don't. You never were a very good liar and you're sticking pretty closely to your story. I just wish it hadn't landed in my lap. I've got plenty to do without this sort of trouble. Anything to do with Lavender is a can of worms. And you know what worms are used for. Bait. How very convenient for Mr Lavender that he's out of town at the moment.'

'Out of town?'

'According to the woman who works at the video arcade he's holidaying at Noosa.'

'No murder reported, no one knows anything, and the boss is away. Doesn't it all seem a bit too convenient?'

'Precisely. Once again as far as Harry Lavender is concerned we are boxing at shadows. He's got more security and protection around him than the Pentagon.'

'Yes, but the Pentagon has been broken into. By a ten-year-old child.'

'You know any children who are going to break Lavender?'

'Maybe.'

She was smiling and shaking her head.

'Go home and get some rest, Claudia. I'll get someone to drive you.'

'Thanks.'

'Don't mention it. And Claudia . . .'

'Yes?'

'Try and stay out of the sort of trouble that brings you to my office.'

'I'll do my best.'

'Claudia, I'm serious. You go after Lavender, you'll get swallowed up without a trace. Leave it alone.'

'Out all night and you arrive home mid-morning in a cop car. There must be a story there.'

'There is, Jack, but after. At the moment I have some pressing business to attend to.'

I looked at the phone and I looked at the bed. The bed won. I could never understand how Philip Marlowe and those guys, from one end of the story to the other, got shot, beaten up, and sometimes laid, without ever going to bed.

I stand on top of my city and see the shape of the future. It is a circuit board, the microchip buildings connected by filament roads. My address in the city is The Beehive. This name is no accident. From the central processing unit I see my empire stretch out. And its form is not unlike that of a beehive, the image of the electronic future. The hexagonal cells store information that feeds the system. A pattern as perfect as a circuit board, the chips themselves like silicon bees relaying information. Like the computer, bees have a binary language system. They dance the information, the direction of the pollen and its distance from the hive. Direction and distance is all they need for their world of honey. The sticky gold that also traps their enemies. My world can be reduced to direction and distance. To a binary system of zeroes and ones. On off. On off. The computer manifests our thought patterns. We cannot help but create in our own image. All artefacts are mirrors.

Drones like Johnny the Jumper are expendable. They are merely acting on genetic orders, following instructions on direction and distance to arrive at the pollen that is transmuted to honey back in the hive. There are thousands like the Jumper. In the world of the hive deviation is not tolerated.

Then there is the queen bee who generates the world of the hive, the motherboard that holds all the other boards that make up the computer box. It holds in its body the heart: the central processing unit. Here instructions are executed, decisions taken and the whole system coordinated. In other parts of the system data can be relocated but never changed. Only in the heart can data be changed.

Especially if the heart has an electronic implant. It all comes down to pulse, the rhythmical throbbing of arteries, the throb of life. And death. The successive contractions of the heart as the electronic pulse is quickened. Just a little at a time. Just enough to keep the subject in a state of 'readiness'. On edge so that when the time comes the heart is in critical condition. *Autopsy would find no suspicious traces. Examination of the pacemaker would reveal a quickened pulse but this would be put down to exertion. Never would they know that the quickening had been controlled and manipulated from the start.*

The motherboard also holds ROM and RAM, Romulus and Remus, the twins suckled in the wild that created the Roman city, the ROM city. RAM is read/write memory. Information can be read out of and written into this memory, and can be changed at any time. ROM is read only memory. You cannot put your own program into ROM: it holds a prerecorded program. With ROM nothing can be written into the memory, it cannot be changed. The motherboard holds the memory of the city. The everchanging program, the buildings, lives, destroyed and created, the new coats of paint over old, the interpretations of history, the overlays. It also holds the unchangeable program, the history etched onto the hologram of time and space, the pattern produced by interference between coherent light-beam and light diffracted.

The motherboard holds the pattern of light that appears on the screen. The flickering dots that form words and images. The signs, the superficialities. The features of the face of the computer, the screen, where the operator can see work in progress. This is a fragile state because nothing is yet recorded, everything is in flux. Messages hover subliminally for a split second and can then be erased. But already the suggestion has been implanted, beyond the surface of the screen, through the optical fibres into the irretrievable limbo files.

The motherboard holds the board which connects to the keyboard and hard-copy terminal. This orchestrates input and output, the fingers tapping keys which translate and translate into the zeroes and ones, the binary system of the computer brain. Then out again, up from the depths of zeroes and ones, translations back up the chain of command to the printer tapping hieroglyphs onto paper.

The motherboard holds the disc controller which allows information to be stored outside the computer, far enough away so that all connections disappear. A disc is a piece of throwaway plastic, precarious as paper and just as easily destroyed, as meaningless as a sheet of music in the hands of a layman, but coaxing and *revealing to the eye attuned to it. The computer eye.*

Regrets? Only one. That I will not live long enough to witness and enjoy the full impact of the electronic future. The horizon stretches infinitely. Technology is light years ahead of ethics. I have extracted more gold from the electronic revolution than from the euphoric flowers of Asia or all the rest of my business interests put together. Ironically the old principles apply: know your terrain, fight with what you've got, slip through the interstices.

The computer game par excellence.

Know the system, slip between the gaps when computer time is suspended. Rearrange a few binary digits. Write a self-destruct clause so that the program deletes itself when the operation is completed. Six million dollars in less than a month. Should my associate in the bank be discovered and the rearrangement traced to him he will probably be promoted. He shows initiative, enterprise, why not give him something more interesting and challenging to do. There will be no prosecution. The bank's security system is inviolable. Money is involved and ethics are deleted. And what has he done after all? The customers' accounts are in order. Has he stolen? A thimbleful of time and electricity. Has he broken and entered? Broken a code and entered a system. There is no damage to property, no loss of life.

My life and the list of my crimes have been long and illustrious. The motherboard could last forever but the casement of flesh is crumbling, dragging down with it the central processing unit as the program runs amok. The chips are down, turned into post holocaust insects running rampant in a system where only insects survive. Uncontrolled growth spreading and recurring.

I will go gently into that dark night, not rage against the dying of the light. I will survive death as I survived the holocaust of childhood. My mountain of gold, my cancerous city, my life and crimes will enter into the unalterable hologram of time and space.

I t was 4pm when I woke up, my body ready for a fresh assault on the concrete and glass jungle but my head not keeping up with it. There were messages on the Ansafone but I was already being bombarded with too much information. My aching head was trying to tell me something.

Something that didn't fit into the pattern. I swallowed some vitamins, a few Panadols, then opened the french doors and breathed in a couple of lungsful of pollution, the breath of the city, of Harry Lavender's city.

That's what didn't fit into the pattern – the overt headache, the cheap thriller violence. Lavender played cat and mouse. Worked on the nerves, seduced the victim into the game, made you think you were ahead when really he was rattling you to death. Pointing the bone and playing on the death wish. He was a legend but he was also a man. The legend was untouchable but the flesh and blood of the man could be pierced. One pebble from a slingshot could hit him right between the eyes. If I could find his eyes, the windows, the grimy shopfront windows to his human soul.

The night at the video arcade was a bad dream. I'd been watched but untouched. Then I'd been clobbered. And set up. Harry Lavender loomed so large but there were other people in the world. Other people who might want to black me out. The Maori for instance. It was the Maori who'd put the lights out for me. Who could see in the dark.

The paranoid makes connections between signs that the 'normal' person doesn't. Everything is grist to the mill.

I am not paranoid, I just have a god-awful headache.

I showered and washed my hair. Washed blood out of it. Swirling down into the bath and away to some point off Bondi.

Bondi and blood.

I couldn't believe Robbie was dealing. Or even using. A one-way street, he'd said. He looked so . . . nice, so clean-cut and fresh.

So had Mark Bannister.

I swallowed hard and turned the taps on full pelt, drowning the blood, my blood, the blood of dead boys, in water.

It felt better. The ionising shower pummelled my head and body. Or maybe it was just the numbing of the Panadol.

I turned on the Ansafone and got the voices of 'normal' people.

First there was Otto. Could I meet him tonight at six? Then there was a voice out of the blue – Mrs Levack, thinking the Ansafone was my secretary and hanging up. I hoped it was for more than just a cup of tea. Then there was Steve Angell.

Steve Angell. Still alive and not hysterical. At least not on the Ansafone. Of all the people who'd had contact with Mark Bannister he was the one I'd seen the most of. How had he managed to slip through the net? What was he trading to save his exquisite skin?

If I could just hear his voice I would know. But I'd just heard his voice and I didn't know. The phone voice wasn't enough. Impersonal. Blanched. I wanted to see him. To forget the lavender cancer growing in my brain. Wanted to drink champagne and watch the dawn. To get drunk, laugh, to be in the sweet embrace and have the earth shift under me, the city shift under me, the continental plates shift and immerse me in deep oceans.

'Steve? It's Claudia.'

He was the same as ever. As if nothing had changed. But something had changed. The magic light of dawn had become a hot burning glare.

'I've been . . . busy.' . . . 'Tonight? I'm not sure . . .' . . . 'Nothing. Everything's fine, just fine.'

My mouth relaxed into a smile. Tonight, he said. Key in the letterbox, champagne in the fridge and hot water in the bath, just in case.

Deep oceans of hot water, champagne, the sweet embrace. How could I ever have doubted him?

'Hmm, sounds great, Steve, I'll be there as soon as I can. See you.'

There was something else.

'Yes?'

He'd just been notified about the death of a patient.

The new recipient of Mark Bannister's pacemaker.

I froze. Hard and cold.

Bloke from Orange. Collided with a semi. The pacemaker was irretrievable.

No way to check now if it had been interfered with. No way at all.

My head started spinning. No, no, this can't be true, no, it is not happening, the coincidences are too great. TERMINAL ILLNESS THE LIFE AND CRIMES OF HARRY LAVENDER. The life terminating illness of the crimes of Harry Lavender.

'Yes. I'm still here. Where do you get the pacemakers, Steve?' I said, spitting out his name. . . . 'Which manufacturers?'

Hartronics. Harry Lavender.

'Thanks, Steve, that's all I wanted to know. And Steve: you can stop bugging me. You're not going to hear anything more on this phone.'

I slammed the phone down and cradled my head in my hands. How could he do it? How could he do it? How could . . . how could . . . I squeezed my eyes tightly shut to stop the wave welling up inside me. But the tears leaked out just the same. Leaked out and ran down my cheeks just as his light feathery touch had done a million years ago. The phone was ringing. And ringing. How could you do it, Steve, how could you do it? The phone rang on and on. But I didn't hear it till it stopped.

'What happened to you? I thought you'd walked out on me as well.'

'What do you mean "as well"?'

'Oh,' Otto began airily, 'I met someone last night, he was supposed to call in on his way home from work. That was two hours ago.' He tsked and rolled his eyes to the ceiling. It all sounded so depressingly familiar.

'Yeah, well, there's a lot of heart breaking going around,' I said glumly. 'Here, this will cheer you up.' And I handed him a bag of croissants.

Otto started nibbling the nuts off a particularly large and sickly-looking almond croissant.

'Aren't you having any?'

'No, I ate something at the pub.' Something hard and indigestible.

'Why do you insist on living at that pub? It must be so . . . unsavoury.'

'It's a nice pub, good clientele. Safety in numbers.'

'You just like it because there are lots of young men around.'

I smiled wryly and sighed. 'C'mon, Otto, let's get on with it. This is going to be a long night.'

'Maybe not, Claudia. It depends how long it takes you to find the password.'

'What do you mean: how long it takes me to find the password? You said you got a positive result on that number I gave you.'

'All that told us was that it's a data transmission number. To open communication you also need a password.'

'Well, program your computer to randomly combine letters.'

'My dear Claudia,' he said wearily. 'That could take weeks. Much as I hate to admit it – and I do not want you spreading this around my shop,' he said, putting his hands over the disc drive so that the computer could not hear, 'there are times when the human brain is more efficient. My computer knows nothing about your Mr Lavender. You have the advantage there. Operators choose a password that has significance for them – the name of their dog, the name of their lover – they don't want something so complicated that they might forget the combination of letters. They want something of significance to them but of little importance to anyone else, something that protects their system from easy access. So you put yourself in the shoes of the person who chose the password. You are an actor playing a character. You walk and talk and breathe that character. Then you'll find the password. It's very simple.'

All very easy for him to say. It was me who had to do it. But I had been preparing for this. Every breath I took reeked of Lavender.

'So I have to randomly select passwords and try them against the numbers.'

'Haven't you been listening? Not randomly select, just try passwords that the operator might think of.'

'That's what I mean.' Knowing the deviousness of Harry Lavender I might as well have been randomly selecting.

There were obvious names. Mark, Sally, perhaps even Harry. I shuddered. Stared at the blank computer, the door into a dark, labyrinthine, subterranean maze, a purgatory you wandered through forever trying to find the way out – and the only way out was death. Human names were too obvious for Lavender. It would be secret, something known only to him. And Mark. A dead man.

But Harry Lavender was the double negative. The negative that became positive. Naming one thing invokes its opposite. Harry Lavender was the extreme of deviousness. And when you went to the extreme of deviousness there was nowhere left to go but the obvious.

When I gained entry, pressed the final key, would lightning bolt up my arm and attack my heart too?

'This is the first step of a descent into hell. Are you ready, Otto?'

Otto was in the passenger's seat now, swallowing the last of the croissant.

I keyed in the number and waited. The brain started ticking, then meaningful dots of light stretched across the screen:

> system ready
> enter password

I was in. Not quite in but I was knocking on the door.

I tried names, every name I could think of. Dogs' names, people's names. Mark, Sally, Harry.

Nothing.

I tried the dollar sign, asterisks, exclamation marks, plus and minus signs.

'More coffee?'

'Thanks,' I said. I rubbed my eyes and temples and stared into the coffee. It was awfully black, like staring into a hole in the road. But a lot better than cops' coffee.

'Don't forget this,' said Otto, lightly touching a key to the left. 'It alters the keyboard completely.'

The paranoid makes connections between signs that the normal person doesn't see. A quantum leap from one matrix to another. Or perhaps an element common to both sets.

I thought of Koestler and *The Act of Creation*. Koestler who, with his wife, had committed suicide rather than die of terminal illness.

The overlapping of matrices. The act of creation occurs when two matrices overlap in the mind. Koestler pushed the theory through puns, the arts, philosophy, science. Archimedes, for example – the water level in the bath must have risen a thousand times. It was only when he had a problem to solve, the weight of silver in that filigreed crown, that his mind started scanning the myriad of phenomena of the world and noticed the rising level of bath water. Not only noticed but Eureka! it gelled. There was an added incentive. Archimedes' head would be on the block if he didn't come up with an answer – a great stimulus for making quantum leaps.

The brain takes in everything and records indiscriminately. It is the rational mind that sorts and sifts. Sends the garbage to the subconscious till the dream man comes along and takes it away. But the mind makes mistakes. Sometimes a perfectly good item is relegated to the dump, and wells up again from subterranean depths. Subterranean, subconscious, subliminal, sub. Lower position, covertness, secrecy, under, under the surface. I had only been trying the overt, the visible letters of the keyboard but underneath each of them was a secret symbol, a subtext. The obvious and the devious.

Alter: change in characteristics, position, change in character.

Altar: a flat-topped box for offerings to deity, Communion table, communication table.

I held my finger on the flat-topped box of the ALT key and tried all the names again. I got some nice looking hieroglyphs but none of them opened the door.

No entry into the sub-world haunted by the shadow of Harry Lavender.

But I hadn't tried everything. I hadn't tried the one word that would gain me entry. The name important to Harry Lavender but of no significance to anyone trying to break into his system. Alter. Reverse the positions, rearrange the words. The positive becomes negative and the negative, positive. The name unimportant to Harry but of full significance to the person trying to break into his system.

In the reflection of the computer screen what I'd been looking for was staring me in the face.

It was my name, my name that was Harry Lavender's password.

I played a symphony. The sinister left hand holding down the ALT chord while the dextrous right keyed in the melody.

It flashed on the screen, the cursor winking furiously.

My palms were sweating. I sat back exhausted with concentration. I looked at Otto and swallowed hard. No words were spoken in that electrifying atmosphere. This is how it must be for bomb disposal squads, tracing the maze of wires leading to the timer, where any false move, a minuscule uncoordination could shatter you into a million pieces. You have to go on, the clock is ticking, you have to touch the next piece, though every instinct in your body is screaming not to, the fingers resisting like magnetic repulsion.

'Open the file, Claudia.'

I didn't move.

'Open the file, Claudia . . . Claudia?'

I shot out of the chair. Reeling from the cattle prod on the back of the neck.

'Claudia! For God's sake!'

It was Otto, only Otto putting his hand on my shoulder.

I stared at the screen.

'There's something wrong. Why is it my name? Why is it my name that opens the door? The book was written before I was even born. Why is my secret name on that screen and that cursor winking, winking, winking at me?'

'People change passwords all the time, to protect themselves. You know that.'

Who is protecting me?

'Yes. I know.' I had nothing to do with the writing of the book but I had everything to do with it now.

The rush was subsiding, the pulse back to normal. The pulse, the electronic pulse of the cursed cursor waiting for me to make the next move.

'Return, Claudia, return.'

The subterranean river of no return.

'I'm too far in now to return.'

'Press RETURN to open the file. How can you sit there staring, Claudia? Aren't you just dying of curiosity?'

Curiosity might kill me.

'This is no ordinary computer game, Otto. I'm about as curious as a bomb disposal squad.'

'What? What's wrong, Claudia? Do you want me to do it?'

'No, Otto, I'll do it.'

Ki energy breathed into the abdomen, the body's centre of gravity.

I RETURNed to open the file, the file of my secret name.

TO MY VALENTINE

Lavender had been guiding me down this path all along. I had been caught up in his maze, looking for the piece of cheese.

The screen filled with red light, red light that finally settled into the shape of a heart. A blood red heart.

Then my heart stopped.

Lavender-coloured crabs crawled down the screen, and where they went nothing was left. TO MY VALENTINE disappeared letter by letter, then the crabs went to work on the heart, eating it bit by bit.

I had stopped breathing. My whole body had stopped. All that was left were eyes. Eyes riveted to the screen.

There were words, far away. '. . . some sophisticated sort of Trojan . . .'

I must have asked what that was because more words floated into my ears.

'. . . Trojan Horse . . . a built-in deleting program . . . normally used to protect copyright . . .'

'What?'

'It usually just wipes everything out. I've never seen crabs before, well, not on a computer screen.'

'What star sign are you Otto?'

'Capricorn. The goat,' he said.

'Do you know what the symbol for Cancer is?'

'Oh,' he said, his voice deflated.

'Yes, the crab. That symbol for cancer has eaten my heart. And has been eating it away right from the beginning!'

The screen now was blank except for the winking cursor.

Everything that ever was or ever could be had been deleted. My past and future obliterated. My heart.

'Playing cat and mouse with my heart,' I said, more to myself than Otto.

'You know what a mouse is in computer jargon?' he said. 'It's the thing that moves the cursor around the screen.'

curse: utterance of deity consigning person or thing to destruction.

curse: excommunication.

cursive: writing done with joined characters.

cursorial: having limbs adapted for running.

cursory: hasty, hurried, going rapidly over something without noticing details.

cursor: a movable reference point, movable to the part of the display where measurements are computed.

The cursor gives your position on the screen. Tells you where you are. *You are the cursed mouse running round in my maze. Recognise this, my child, you are in my maze, in the very heart of it. All the exits have been blocked off, your little nose is quivering, soon you will be gasping for air. But it will be too late, I have cut off all the life support systems and you will suffocate in my embrace.*

But there was still the piece of cheese and Lavender wanted that cheese as much as the mouse. He wasn't playing dead men's games for the fun of it. I was looking for something that he wanted. Something that he'd obliterated, deleted from his life but hadn't been able to obliterate from Mark's.

Once again I was standing on the edge of the blue light. I had to draw the cat out of his hidey-hole. I wanted him to know I knew what he was looking for. And wanted so badly he would go to any lengths to get it. Including keeping me alive till I had found it.

I played my hunch and entered into that blank file THE LIFE AND CRIMES OF HARRY LAVENDER.

Returned his service. All I had to do now was keep the volley going and never let the ball fall on the ground. If the ball fell to the ground I'd be dead.

Otto looked at me aghast. 'What did you do that for? We could have quietly switched off and no one would be any the wiser.'

The words queued up and filed out of my mouth like strangers. 'I want him to know that I have cracked his system. That I have played his deathly game and am not afraid.'

Like the suicide is not afraid of death.

'Well then,' said Otto with the flippancy of mania, 'anything else you'd like to say while we're at it?'

'No,' I said coldly.

I walked out of the shop. It was night and the lights were on in Harry Lavender's city, neon signs winking like the cursed cursor. It was not a late night shopping night and the city was dead. The lights were on but all the doors were closed.

I could not go home. Not follow a path that Harry Lavender knew. He was not the omnipotent eye of God, just a smart, devious fellow. Dying of cancer, the brain addled, he would make mistakes.

Mrs Levack. No message on the Ansafone. An unwittingly smart move. On a bugged phone no news is good news.

I was itchy. Ran my fingers throught my hair. Felt under my arms, examined my clothes for bugs. I was clean. I knew I was clean. Clean and just a little bit paranoid. I turned it into an advantage. The adrenalin of paranoia became alertness, super-awareness. Harry Lavender was just a man.

I was about to hail a cab then thought better of it. The ghost of Ronny O'Toole could be driving a cab that just happened by.

I caught the bus to Bondi. Right to the Esplanade. Far away enough to sniff out a tail as I walked the dark streets to the Levacks', blending into the shadows.

She'd taken the rollers out of her hair. Blonde hair that was grey at the roots.

'Miss Valentine!'

Mr Levack was sitting with his head in the paper but he managed a small sign of recognition.

'You rang me, Mrs Levack. Sorry I wasn't there to take the message personally.'

A frown manifested from the wrinkles of Mrs Levack's forehead. 'Your secretary seemed such a quiet girl, not very talkative at all. I asked if I could talk to you but she didn't say anything.'

'It's my Ansafone, Mrs Levack, you just leave messages on it. Like a tape recorder.'

Mr Levack put the paper down on the coffee table. 'I told her it was one of them answering services but she insisted that someone had spoken to her. Sometimes I think Mavis lives in another century.'

I was in no mood for small talk.

'What did you ring about, Mrs Levack?'

'This, dear.' She handed me a letter addressed to Mark Bannister. A letter from America. 'I know I shouldn't of done it, taking mail out of letter boxes, but it was sticking out. See it's one of them long envelopes and . . . if I knew his next of kin I would of given it to them but you were the only one I could think of.'

'It was all I could do to stop her steaming it open,' threw in Mr Levack.

'It might be important, dear. Aren't you going to open it?'

It was a toss up who was more curious: Mrs Levack or me.

On the top left hand corner of the envelope was the name Grosz, Grosz and Epstein and a New York address.

I opened it.

```
Dear Mark Bannister,
   Thank you for sending us 'The Life and Crimes
of Harry Lavender'. You are a talented writer
but I'm afraid this one's not for us. There
were some good touches here and there but the
writing is, we think, slightly overdone and
there doesn't seem to be any plot. I am sure
that you will find somebody to take it but I
don't think that we are the people.
   Awaiting your further instructions re return
of disk.

Yours
```

Nancy Grosz

```
Nancy Grosz
```

Too late and too early to ring the States, so near and yet so far.

'When did you pick this up, Mrs Levack?'

'Just today, dear. I rang you as soon as possible.'

'Ever since you came here the first time she's been snooping around. Thinks she's Angela Lansbury,' scoffed Mr Levack.

I could have kissed her. A nice normal nosy parker, the sort of person a man like Harry Lavender in his world of manipulators and manipulatees doesn't take into account.

'You're a jewel, Mrs Levack. I don't know how to thank you.'

She went all fluffy, like a little girl in her first party dress.

'Don't go telling her things like that,' said the voice of reason. 'She'll never get her hat on the way her head's swelling out.'

'Oh shut up, Eddy! Just go back to reading the paper,' she said, heady with power. 'Claudia,' she said confidentially, 'that letter, ahem, is it important?'

'It's just a letter from a publisher. Would you like to read it?'

Would she like to read it! Is the Pope Polish?

Her eagle eyes moved along the lines, her mouth shaping the words.

'Oh, the poor thing, all that writing and they didn't want it. Oh, the poor thing. I knew he was a writer, though. Didn't I say he was a writer?'

'You thought he was a student,' said Mr Levack. 'It's not the same thing.'

Right now he could slide into the woodwork and Mrs Levack wouldn't even notice.

'That girl's been round again,' she said knowingly. 'Took all his personal belongings away. She was looking for something in the flat, too. Like the man in the driving gloves. Had one of them fancy cars . . .'

'Porsche, it was a Porsche, a black one. Very flash.'

'Been back since, too. But she can't get in any more because new people have moved in, a nice young couple, the girl sings while she's doing the cleaning and the young man wears a suit when he goes to work.' A whole new mini-series for Mrs Levack to watch. '*She,* that other girl, she was looking in the letter box one day. That's what gave me the idea to do it.'

'Ha!' snorted Mr Levack. 'You don't need any excuses to go looking through people's mail.'

'I didn't even open the box, Eddy, it was sticking out the slot.'

'Humph!'

I stood up. 'I'll be in touch, Mrs Levack, Mr Levack.' I smiled.

'If anything else . . . crops up, Mrs Levack, don't hesitate to call.'

I hoped she looked in her own letter box as often as she looked in other people's.

Because next time she did she'd find a sheet of Instant Lotto tickets. Good luck, Mrs Levack.

'**S**ally? It's Claudia.' At the other end was cold silence. I wasn't really expecting flowers and chocolate.

'Are you there, Sally?' I was surprised the telephone didn't seize up considering the amount of ice being poured into it. 'I want to talk to you.'

She didn't want to talk to me, a jagged edge to her voice now, the Sally I knew and didn't love so well.

'You talk to me or you talk to the cops. Take your pick.' . . . 'Something of great interest to you. I'm sure you don't want to discuss it over the phone.' . . . 'No, not your place or mine. How do you fancy a sauna?' . . . 'I said a sauna. Women only, no men around, especially nasty men with guns.'

I gave her the address in the city. It was private and would put a damper on her hysteria. And it might just sweat out the truth.

From the public phone box I called Brian Collier. And Otto, who was home now, drinking a few ports to get over the excitement of the evening. I rang Carol but she wasn't there. I thought better of leaving a message. Too soon for her bungling boys to appear on the scene. Besides, as long as I knew where the manuscript was and no one else did I had a life assurance policy. I stuck the envelope back down, readdressed Mark's letter to myself c/o the pub's P.O. Box and popped it in the nearest mailbox. Then walked down to the bus stop.

The bus, when it finally arrived, trundled past the street where the mailbox was. I took one last look and smiled. A van was there and they were emptying the box. The letter would arrive safe and sound in the morning.

Then I stopped smiling. Last clearance was at 6 pm and it was way past six.

The businesswomen who usually used the gym were long since gone. I got a towel from Margaret and sat in the reception area drinking coffee.

Sally walked in five minutes later carrying a bag full of stuff and looking like she'd wandered in the wrong door.

She wasn't smiling. Neither was I.

I signed her in.

The small talk was exceedingly small.

'Are your parents back from overseas yet?'

'End of the week.'

I guided Sally past the mirrors into the spa and sauna area.

It was semi-dark and smelled of warm timber and we were alone.

We undressed slowly, watching each other like strippers, then wrapped our respective towels up under our armpits and went into the sauna. I shut the door tightly behind us. I didn't want her running out on me now. Not now that she was here. How easily she had come – seemingly unaccompanied.

'I love saunas,' she said, stretching her arms out along the bench. 'Sooo relaxing.' Her towel crept down a few centimetres, revealing plump breasts and halfmoons of dark brown nipples. She subtly moved her body, causing the towel to drop away completely.

But I wasn't falling for it.

'Why did you give me the run-around about the computer?'

She sat up, startled. 'What do you mean?'

I moved close to the door, blocking her only escape route.

'I mean why did you give me the run-around about the computer?'

Her tongue peeped out of her slightly opened mouth and licked little beads of moisture from her lips.

'I . . . I don't know what you're talking about.'

'You do know. No nasty men came with guns after my last visit, did they? You just wanted me off your back. Didn't want me coming back with any computer experts. Afraid an expert might be able to wheedle something out of the computer that you couldn't.'

She stood up, wrapping the towel around her. 'I have to have a shower.'

'Sit down.'

'You're holding me against my will. I'll scream the place down if you don't let me go.'

I shoved her back on the bench. Sweat was pouring from both of us. It would be slippery wrestling with her but I would if I had to.

'Scream all you like, sweetheart. No one will come, it's only you and me.'

Her eyes scanned the timber box, darting like a mouse in a maze while the cat held its paw over the door.

'There are no monitoring screens in here, the door has no lock apart from me and I'll put a headlock on you if necessary.'

'What if I faint?' she said pathetically.

'You faint, I take you out and stick you under a cold shower then I bring you back in again. As many times as is necessary.'

Cold hard bitch, cold hard monster.

'You're a woman! How can you talk like that!' Then she changed tack. 'Claudia ... Claudia, can't we ...?' Her eyes groping in my heart for the soft spots. I had a lock on them too.

'I'm doing a job. It gets a bit messy at times but then I deal with messy people.' Cold hard renunciation.

For the sake of their craft the Amazons cut off the breast closest to the heart.

'Why are you here, Sally? You could easily have just not come. I didn't exactly frogmarch you into here. Why did you come?'

'Please, Claudia, I'm going to faint.'

'First tell me why you came.'

'How can I tell you anything if I'm lying on the ground?'

'Lying is what you do best,' I spat at her.

We were both breathing heavily, breathing in each other's thick expelled air. I didn't know how much longer I could last either.

I opened the door. 'Shower.'

She unwound her towel and staggered to the shower. I stood

155

ten centimetres away from her, the secondhand spray dampening my towel, cooling my head.

She ran shivering to her bag.

'What are you doing?'

'Just getting my bathrobe. That towel's all wet.'

She put it on, wrapped the towelling sash around her waist and stuck her hands into the deep pockets.

'Better?' I asked sarcastically.

'Much.'

'Now, will you tell me why you came?'

My eyes never left hers. We were holding each other's eyes in a throttling lock.

'I've come for my book.'

My eyes dropped. Down to my stomach, or where my stomach should have been. My insides curdled and all of time eclipsed into the barrel of the gun she had aimed at my navel. Just a small gun, the sort women in New York carry as protection against rapists. A close range gun, the bullet ready to rupture my umbilical cord and dissever me from life.

'Your book? I thought it was Mark's book.'

'He dedicated it to me. It's my book and I want it back.'

'Pull that trigger and you'll never find it.'

'I didn't want it found.' She smiled triumphantly. 'But you had to go and find it, didn't you? That's why you called me here, isn't it, because you've found it?'

In the endless silence of the room my mind chattered like a chipmunk, deftly darting here and there looking for a way out of the maze. Alter. Reverse positions. Now I was the mouse. She had me over a barrel, a small one but at this range very effective. This was a child holding me to ransom. Cute, flighty, and ultimately dangerous. A child who'd have to be handled with kid gloves. Any untimely move and the highly strung nerves would jerk the trigger.

I dragged my eyes away from the gun and up towards hers. Up so the eyes didn't know what the legs had planned. Too close to run now but close enough to . . . 'Yes, I've found it.'

'Where is it?'

'In my bag. I'll get it.'

'Don't move.'

She circled around me, gun aimed higher now, at the heart.

Left hand felt for my bag, took it off the hook, unbuckled, felt inside the bag. She would feel the shape of my cassette recorder. Thicker, but not unlike a disc. The momentary flicker of eyes. The hand emerging now, holding it. The flicker again. Shadow of dismay.

'Hua!' My legs went into action, paralysing the wrist and knocking the gun into the shower recess. She dived for it. So did I, the towel and modesty now forgotten. She got to it first but couldn't curl her fingers round it. I wrenched her up by the back of the bathrobe and threw her onto the tiles. She was panting with frustration, fighting back the tears. She had landed on her coccyx, her eyes screwed up with pain, still fighting, fighting the tears.

I had the gun now and she was coming up. Slow motion. I flung open the door of the sauna and threw the gun in. She came for it then saw where it had landed: in the fire box of electric coals.

'Any more bright ideas, sweetheart?'

She flopped down on the bench, left hand holding the paralysed right wrist, chest heaving heavily, revving up, revving up.

She came at me with the full force of animal survival, trying to push me against the fire box.

I dodged. She ran smack into the wall and teetered back bewildered. She made for the open door of the sauna. I grabbed her hair and reeled her back.

She was hysterical now and screaming, wild-eyed, savage. I raised my hand to hit her across the face.

'Not my face! Don't hit my face! Don't hit my face!'

She buried her face in the folds of her bathrobe, protecting her pride and joy.

I dropped my hand.

'Claudia? Are you still in there? We're closing up now.'

It was Margaret.

'God! What's . . . ?'

'Call the cops, Margaret. Central. Get them to page Detective

157

Carol Rawlins. Tell her I'm having another tea party, would she like to join me.'

It didn't matter whether she got onto Carol or not. What mattered was that Sally heard it.

'You've got about fifteen minutes to save your life and this time it better be the real version. That gun will be red hot by then and they'll want to know what an illegal fire-arm is doing in your possession.'

She was still whimpering into her bathrobe.

I jerked her head up.

'No, no! Don't touch my face! You bitch! I did it for my father! For my father!'

'You were the delivery girl, were you? Waiting till your father had reduced me to a screaming heap then you were to come in and pick up the pieces.'

'My father's done nothing to you.' Her eyes searched my face. 'My father's a good man.'

'Your father's slime. Don't give me that good man stuff. He killed your boyfriend, for God's sake! Or was that all part of the set-up?'

'Daddy wasn't even here when Mark died. What are you talking about?'

'Don't do it, Sally, just don't do it. You've got ten minutes now and when the police get here and start asking you questions they won't be worrying about your pretty little face!'

'Claudia, Claudia . . . my father left me the gun when he went away. Self-protection. I was in a big house all by myself. I . . . I . . .'

'Don't waste your ten minutes on the gun, I want to hear the rest, all of it. You can start with what you were coincidentally doing at Mark's flat when he was having his heart attack.'

'I told you! The studio cancelled so I came back to the flat.'

'Yes, you did tell me,' I said through clenched teeth. 'Now you can tell me what you *did* there.'

'I . . . I . . . didn't do anything.'

'Yes, you did. You did do something. You went into the bathroom.'

'I . . . I went to the toilet.'

'You went to the toilet.' My voice was thick with sarcasm. 'At a time like that? Even if you're busting, the last thing you think of when your boyfriend's lying dead or dying on the floor is going to the toilet.' . . . *it wasn't the stuff it was safe* . . . *some junkie paraphernalia in a plastic bag in the* . . . A wicked smile spread across my face. 'Of course. You did go to the toilet. But it wasn't to relieve yourself. You went to get the *stuff* and you came back and shot Mark up. Why did you shoot him up? To give him a good send-off? Why, Sally, *why*?'

'Because . . . because . . . I told you, I did it for my father. I wanted them to think it was the smack, I didn't want them to think it was the pacemaker.'

'What made you think it was the pacemaker?'

I wrenched her up, her head turning away to avoid the words I was spitting at her. 'What made you think it was the pacemaker?'

'The computer,' she said in a hoarse whisper.

'What?'

'I said the computer!'

I released her and she clumped down on the bench.

She was swallowing air, her chest heaving under the bathrobe.

'It . . . it . . . a message on the computer described a way of killing someone by altering his pacemaker.' She breathed in and tossed her damp hair back. 'It described exactly how it had been done. Mark got his pacemaker checked from home. You connect the tester to the modem and the heartbeat pattern is transmitted to the hospital. But the computer . . . the computer was also connected to the modem. And the computer of the person who sent the message. Someone had put a program into the computer that corrupted the pacemaker program. Mark's was programmed in a special way. The new program altered that. It said the time had come to put the heart in critical condition. So if Mark exerted himself, or got stressed, or did anything that made his heart beat fast he would die. And something did happen to make his heart beat fast. He read his own death. The shock of reading his own death killed him! The message said that a dangerous program had been tried on Mark in the testing period. It said it was on Dr Villos' records. How could

159

I call the police? It implicated my father!'

'The whole book implicated your father! The title implicated your father: "The Life and Crimes of Harry Lavender"! Harry Lavender's your father, isn't he? Isn't he!' Clutching the thin shoulders under the absorbent towelling. The thud, thud, thud of them against the warm dull timber.

'Not Harry Lavender. God, not Harry Lavender!' she spat. 'Raymond Villos is my father.'

The sweaty silence penetrated my brain.

My fingers went limp, my strength sapped. Her thin shoulders slipped away. I flopped back, wiping my arm across my forehead, wiping the sweat out of my brain.

'Why does Harry Lavender have a photo of you?'

She was shaking her head in dismay. She swallowed. 'I . . . I don't know.'

'Because he's your father, isn't he? Isn't he!' Looming over the pretty face, the menace of bodily hurt.

'No, no, Harry Lavender is not my father. Raymond Villos is my father. Harry Lavender is my father's patient.'

'How well do you know him?'

'Know who?'

'Harry Lavender,' I snarled, 'who else?'

'Not very well. Sometimes I looked after reception and I'd see him. He was nice to me, asked me what I was doing, if I had a boyfriend, what my boyfriend did, stuff like that. He told me I had a pretty face, said I should try modelling. Introduced me to an agency.'

'Harry Lavender doesn't do favours without favours being returned. What were you doing for him in return for him setting you up in modelling?'

'Nothing,' she said with the innocence of childhood. 'I didn't have to do anything. What sort of person are you? Can't you believe people can help you without wanting anything in return?'

'Not people like Harry Lavender. There's only one reason he'd do something for you without you being in his debt. It's because he's your father!'

'Why do you keep saying that? He's not my father, he's not!'

'Do you know he's got cancer?'

She nodded her head, a nod so deliberate and long her whole body started slowly rocking.

'Answer me,' I said, going for the face again. 'Do you know he's got cancer?'

'Yes!' she spat. 'I know.'

'Then why was he seeing Dr Villos? Cancer's not his field, he's a heart specialist. OK, so maybe he had pains in the chest, but after the initial visit he needn't have come back. But he did come back. He came back to see you!'

She was panting now, opening and closing her mouth like she wanted to vomit. Her eyes and nose were running, running down her face and joining the rivers of sweat.

I wiped my forehead with the back of my hand, a useless gesture in the sweat box that blurred the edges of us both.

Words came out of the mouth, words I hadn't even thought of, suspended in the heavy liquid air.

'Lavender cancelled your modelling session that day. He wanted you back at Mark's flat to read a message on that screen. Apart from describing Mark's death it said something else, didn't it?'

Her eyes were rolling now, the head loose on its axis.

'Answer me, damn you, answer!'

Her voice came from somewhere far away, as if she had pondered the question for a long, long time and still not found the answer.

'It said that I was his . . . his . . . his . . .' Her mouth couldn't form the shape of the word.

'Daughter.'

She dug deep for her last bit of strength, the last thing she could hold onto. 'Yes, that's what it said but it's not true. He only said it to scare Mark more. He said it was funny Mark had dedicated the book to me because I was his daughter. But he couldn't be my father, he couldn't't!'

My voice was quiet now. 'What was it about the manuscript you didn't want found? You were prepared to kill me for it. You wanted it back as much as Lavender.'

'I told you. Because it implicated my father.'

'You've forgotten something, Sally. That bit you saw on the

screen wasn't part of the book. Mark had finished the book. But the book hadn't quite finished Mark. You didn't want the manuscript found not because it implicated your father but because it told the whole world who your real father was! You've got a lot in common with your father. You know what the final irony is? Both of you wanted the book back and you were both prepared to kill for it. For a book that the publishers rejected.'

'He's not my father. He's not! How many more times do I have to tell you!'

'It's yourself you're trying to convince, Sally, not me.'

How many times had I screamed like this, pulled away from my mother when finally she told me my father was like those old men in the park. Sally was denying her father like I'd denied mine. Both of us denying these men who had spawned us.

I felt sympathy for her but it was too late. She and her father had done too much to me and mine for forgiveness. She would survive. And make a name for herself. Whichever name she chose. She was a child of this city.

The child of Harry Lavender.

There was a knocking on the door of the change rooms.

'Just a minute,' I called. 'I think we'd better get dressed, Sally. Sounds like we've got visitors.'

The perplexed child appeared again, the child who had held a lethal toy on me what seemed an eternity ago, the child who had played elastics and had eventually been tripped up.

Now the question marks had been fired into my eyes.

We dressed slowly, eyeing each other, strippers in reverse.

She put make-up on, painted a red smiling mouth, drew lines that defined the beautiful dark eyes.

'Are you ready?'

Sally nodded.

I opened the door and let in the outside world.

C arol was in street clothes, flanked by two uniformed female colleagues.

'Every time I see you lately, Claudia, you're wet.'

'Someone in this city has to stay clean.'

Carol ignored my comment.

'The receptionist informs us you're having a tea party.'

'You've missed most of it. There's only dregs left.'

'Who's your friend, Claudia?'

'This is the child who's going to break Lavender. This is Sally Villos, Harry Lavender's daughter.'

Sally didn't even say hello. Just smiled her defiant painted smile at Carol.

When Carol's eyebrows returned to their normal position her eyes narrowed. 'What happened to your hand?'

'I . . . I fell over. The floor was slippery.'

Then Carol turned to me and sighed. 'I can't hold her for being someone's daughter, even if it is Harry Lavender.'

'Getting pressure from above, eh Carol?'

'What are you talking about?'

The policewomen shifted uncomfortably in their big shoes.

'One of your superiors threatening you with a country posting if you make any moves towards Lavender?'

'What's happened to you, Claudia? Are you so deep in dirt you can't see anything else?'

What was happening to me? I had a lump of steel where the heart should be, I was accusing everyone of working for Lavender, even the angels, I'd beaten up a woman who was no more than a child. I'd done my job. Right to the bitter end. I had made the hard choices, left my children, honed myself down. The Amazon. No breast, no heart.

The girl's smile was smug now, watching the discord between Carol and me. She knew who she was and she was untouchable. One of her powerful fathers would get her off, have a few words to the right people. She would be successful, one way or another, in this beautiful corrupt city.

'Are you laying charges?'

'Yeah, I'm laying charges. She . . .'

BANG! BANG! BANG!

The sauna room exploded.

Then I exploded. Into laughter. I laughed uncontrollably till the tears ran down my legs.

I began trying to shape the laughter into words.

'She pulled a gun on me. Can't you hear the shots?'

Carol signalled the two policewomen to go and attend to it.

'Here,' I said, throwing them my towel, 'you'll probably need this.'

'Claudia, if I could think of some charge to lock you up with I would. Bring yourself down to the station tomorrow morning and make a statement. In the meantime just get out of my hair and don't call me. I don't care if it's rape, murder or genocide, just don't call me. OK?'

'OK, Carol,' I said, still trying to stifle the laughter.

I said goodnight to Margaret and left the change rooms, leaving the mess for Carol to clean up. Carol's authoritative voice echoed down the mirrored corridor: 'Now then, Ms Villos, how do you happen to have an illegal firearm in your possession?'

How can you do it, Carol? How can you do that with a straight face?

The city was quiet. A fine, misty rain was sweeping the streets. Everything smelled fresh and clean. Carol's driver was sitting in the police car munching a hamburger, holding it in the bag still and taking large bites. I said good evening to him on my way past. He looked surprised, nearly startled, a nice boy whose mum had probably warned him about talking to strange women. I walked past the Queen Victoria Building majestic in the rain, its warm, pink, arcade lights like jewels in the crown, towards the cab rank in Park Street.

Of course there were no cabs to be seen, or any other vehicles, except a van that loomed out of the darkness of a side street. As I was about to cross the road it suddenly gathered speed and headed straight for me. I'd seen that van before. At the mailbox. I turned and ran back down George Street. The van spun around and pelted down the street after me.

The police car driver had scrunched up his hamburger bag and was about to drop it on the ground when I flung open the passenger's door.

'Drive!'

'What?'

'Just drive!'

'But . . . but . . . what about Detective Rawlins?'

'I'm working with Detective Rawlins. Now move before the bastard rams us!'

He moved. Hard and fast and just in time.

I turned around and beyond the glare of the van's headlights saw Carol stepping out onto the street with Sally and the policewomen.

'Keep going!' I shouted, as the driver slowed.

'But the lights are red.'

'So? You think that's going to stop *them*?'

I'd made a mistake getting into a car with a law-abiding policeman. I had to get out and use my best weapon, my feet.

But not yet, the van was too close.

'Turn right into York Street.'

'But it's one-way.'

'It'll be dead-end if you don't. Now move!'

He put his foot down and round the corner we went, skidding on the greasy road. The van didn't follow.

'Good. I think we've lost him.'

But we hadn't. The van had cut through the Queen Victoria Building and was heading straight for us.

'Accelerate! Down the car park ramp!'

When we got into the darkness of the underground car park I opened the door. 'Thanks for the ride. Here's $50. Give the bastards a run for my money.'

He drove up the second ramp and disappeared. I waited under cover till the van also went up the ramp. Then I ran. I had to get through to America and get through before Lavender did. I ran down Market Street, following the Monorail and the sign pointing to Darling Harbour.

In the misty rain a tall-masted vintage yacht was slowly heading towards Cockle Bay. I ran up the wide pedestrian walkway across Darling Harbour. Then I heard it. The van, right behind me. In front of me was something I'd never seen before – a closed gate. Then I remembered that in this city of facades, part of the walkway had been a bridge, Pyrmont Bridge. I climbed through the gate just as the van came to a screeching halt.

A door slammed and I looked behind. The Maori was lumbering towards me. In his hand I saw the glint of a knife. Involuntarily I bit my tongue. O'Toole's dead body flashed before me, his hand, his hand holding his . . . I felt sick, everything started swaying. But it wasn't just me. The ground was moving. The bridge was opening to let the yacht through. It was so close I could nearly touch it.

I couldn't go back. I had to keep running forward. The man in the control tower was gesticulating wildly but I had to go on. I could feel the Maori behind me, feel his hot, panting breath. I could see the water now in the ever-widening gap.

Concentration of mind, body and spirit to a point of bright light, a point far beyond the gap. I leaped, airborne, flying through space, watching the gap widen still further. Then down, down I came, down to the ground on the other side, clinging to it like a baby to its mother.

Behind me I heard a shout. I turned and saw the Maori flying through the air towards me. Down, down he came, down short of the safety of the other side, falling like a rock into the waters of Darling Harbour.

'**W**hy Mark Bannister? That's what I'd like to know. Lavender could have paid the best writer in the country to write his memoirs. Anyone would jump at the chance.'

'Don't tell me you're peeved, Brian Collier. You never know, you might get a mention,' I said, grinning at him. 'Anyway, you're alive and Mark's not. He jumped at the chance. Jumped right out of his skin.' I was sitting on Collier's desk, leaning forward. 'You know how Lavender plays his cat and mouse game. He needed a loophole. Needed someone he could play on, someone expendable. It didn't matter that it was his daughter's boyfriend. Fathers aren't always fond of their daughters' boyfriends. He found out he was dying of cancer, a matter of months. He'd built an empire in this city, but that wasn't enough for Lavender. The dying man wanted a written record, wanted to explain himself to posterity, tell the world about his life and crimes.'

'OK, so he picks an unknown. But why kill him? Why bite the hand that's writing the memoirs?'

'Memoirs are accounts of people's lives but Lavender hadn't finished his life when Mark finished his book. Lavender thought he'd be dead by the time the book was finished. That it would be published posthumously. But he wasn't. People with cancer sometimes linger on for years, despite what the doctors say. So what was he going to do? There was a manuscript around that exposed him, and a writer who knew everything. He couldn't take the chance that someone who knew every intimate detail of his life might shoot his mouth off. He kept an eye on him, through Sally, asked her what her boyfriend was doing, what he was up to. He would have been able to tell by Sally's reaction whether she knew anything, and if Mark was going to talk it would be to the person closest to him. It was OK while the book was in progress but as it was nearing completion Mark was getting jumpy. Lavender couldn't trust Mark if he was like that. And besides, there was the heroin. Lavender's heroin. Mark had told people he was writing a book for someone, but he didn't say who. But he must have got greedy – finished the book off himself and put his own name to it. And sent it off to America. The bloody irony of it is that the manuscript was rejected. What time is it, Brian?'

'12.45.'

In a quarter of an hour the publishing houses of America would be open for business. I had to be first cab off the rank. I'd tried international enquiries for Nancy Grosz's home number but it was unlisted.

'And where do you fit into all of this?'

'I was the bunny who had to find the manuscript. The copy Harry hadn't managed to get rid of. He'd wiped it off the hard disc of Mark's computer, but he couldn't be sure there wasn't a copy somewhere, especially as he'd sent O'Toole around to pick up the loose threads, or rather the loose discs and hadn't found it amongst them. It'd draw too much heat if Lavender looked for it himself. He'd put the hard word down through the network but no one knew a thing. He had some time, then. He was safe for a while, at least here. So he engineered a little game. He sent that first cryptic clue to Mark's sister. And then he just sat back and waited. Watched and waited. Chuckling at the irony, that the person Marilyn had chosen for the job was the daughter of the man he'd turned into a derelict. Then when I got off the track and went up the back alleys he sent me the second clue, guided me back onto the right track, right into the heart. What are you grinning at?'

'All this time you were working for Lavender too.'

'**N**ancy Grosz, please.' . . . 'It's Claudia Valentine, from Australia.'

There were chime bells, then Nancy Grosz identified herself.

'Yes, hello, Claudia Valentine here, calling from Australia. I'm investigating a deceased estate. Mark Bannister. I believe he sent you a manuscript on computer disc, *The Life and Crimes of Harry Lavender*. You sent him a rejection slip with a note saying the manuscript would be forwarded separately, on receipt of his further instructions. Do you still have the disc with you?'

She asked me to repeat the author's name and manuscript title. Would I hold or would I like her to call me back?

I looked at Collier. 'I'll hold.'

I got chimes again, an eternity of chimes, ringing like the gates of heaven. We waited, Brian furiously smoking cigarettes, waiting for the story of the century.

'Yes?' I couldn't wipe the grin off my face. 'I'm instructed by the executors of the estate to have the manuscript returned as soon as possible.' ... 'I don't think that would be soon enough. We need to access it urgently and our problem is that we've had a major malfunction. It seems that yours is the only copy. Would it be possible to return it via modem to our computer here?' ... 'Yes? Great!'

I gave her Brian's number and password. Repeated it so she could write it down.

She'd have it sent directly. I praised God for American efficiency. Then I winced at the 'Have a nice day.' Why did the efficiency have to be tinged with such crass ethnocentrism? It wasn't even day here.

I hung up and made an 'o' with my thumb and index finger. 'It's in the bag.'

'Don't put your skates on yet, Claudia. Tomorrow morning when that story hits the stands all hell will break loose. And what about Lavender? If he's been following your progress so carefully he must know you're onto it now. What'll you do when he comes to collect?'

'He'll never find me. I'm going on holidays, as you suggested. Far away from the dirt of Harry Lavender's city. To the land where the palm trees grow. Is there a phone around here I can use?'

The newsroom was full of phones.

'Take your pick.'

I picked one far enough away to give me privacy. Besides, the phone on Brian Collier's desk had just started to ring.

I dialled the number and waited. And waited.

'Steve? Sorry to ring you this late.' . . . 'No, it's not all right. I think I owe you an apology.' . . . 'For the other day, no, for today, so much has happened it seems like years ago. I'm sorry about what I said to you.' . . . 'Pressure, that's all, pressure. Sometimes the job gets . . . out of control.' I chewed away at my bottom lip. 'And so do I.' . . . 'There's something going on here, I'll tell you about it later. Tomorrow's the weekend, what are you doing?' . . . 'Yeah? A week off? Terrific! Ever been to Queensland?' . . . 'Like to go again? You can meet my kids.' . . . 'I'll be over as soon as I can.' . . . 'Yeah, I remember: in the letterbox.' . . . 'Yeah, in the fridge. See you, Steve.' . . . 'Me too.'

Brian was just putting the phone down when I got back to his desk.

'I'm glad you're smiling,' he said, 'because I've got some news for you. Lavender's in a coma. He's not expected to last the night.'

The news pushed me into a sitting position and wiped the smile off my face.

'Well, that's . . . that's . . .' I threw my hands out helplessly and slowly shook my head. I didn't know whether to laugh or cry. The man who perpetrated his life and crimes through technology now depended on technology for his very breath. I had him, had him in the palm of my hand. And he'd slipped away.

'One more day. Just one more day. Why couldn't the bastard have stayed conscious for just one more day?'

'It's been Harry's game all along. His memoirs will be made public after he's gone, just as he intended. Look on the bright side, Claudia. You're lucky. He can't touch you now.'

'Oh no?'

I slid off the desk, walked past all the monitors receiving news of the city, and stood at the window looking at the city herself. *Her far horizons, her jewelled sea, her beauty and her terror . . .* In the distance was the city's glory, the bright arc of the Bridge curving into darkness, the shimmering star-struck waters of the harbour, the reflection of it in the city's tall glass mirrors. All around the city lights were winking in conspiracy. I looked down below to street level. A drunk was pissing in the doorway of a pub. In another doorway a dero was nestled in for the night, nestled into the newspapers emanating from this building. It could have been Guy, it didn't matter any more. He was just part of the city, like all of us. Part of Harry Lavender's city.

My city was the most beautiful harbour in the world, a childhood of open doors, of ocean breezes on hot summer nights, of passionfruit and choko vines growing in the heart of a city without pollution, the innocence of a time past, before the stench of Lavender. But the stench had always been there, I just hadn't smelled it till there was no place left that didn't reek of it.

Except for museum pieces most of my city had been annihilated in the changing facades, its soul gutted, leaving as much life in it as in a taxidermist's workshop.

Annihilated by men making their own history. Men who uprooted trees to decorate their edifices, levelled people's homes to construct monuments to themselves, concrete and glass monuments reflecting their own images.

As long as the innocent bystanders were untouched we turned a blind eye to it. But the bystanders are touched. And we are not innocent. Secretly we admire men like Lavender. We cut down tall poppies but we let the cancer run rampant.

The big fish get away.

Slip and slide in the waters that nourish them.

'Claudia!'

It was Collier, calling me back to his desk.

'It's coming through now. You've missed the dedication.' To the child who would inherit this beautiful corrupt city. I was watching the computer. A dull click like something shuffling into gear, then the high-pitched whirr of the printer, the machinery so much a part of Harry Lavender's city.

I dream of funerals. My own. It is a state occasion and I am laid out in the open box moving slowly through the streets of Sydney. The buildings are tall reflective glass. It is my image that is reflected in that glass.

My eyes followed the dots, eating, devouring them, the dots that became letters that became words that became sentences, paragraphs that became **The Life and Crimes of Harry Lavender.**